LEAVING
FISHERS

MARGARET PETERSON
HADDIX

LEAVING
FISHERS

SIMON & SCHUSTER BFYR

NEW YORK LONDON TORONTO SYDNEY NEW DELHI

An imprint of Simon & Schuster Children's Publishing Division
1230 Avenue of the Americas, New York, New York 10020

For information about special discounts for bulk purchases, please contact Simon & Schuster Special Sales at 1-866-506-1949 or business@simonandschuster.com.
The Simon & Schuster Speakers Bureau can bring authors to your live event. For more information or to book an event, contact the Simon & Schuster Speakers Bureau at 1-866-248-3049 or visit our website at www.simonspeakers.com.
Book design by Hilary Zarycky
The text for this book is set in New Caledonia.
Manufactured in the United States of America
This SIMON & SCHUSTER BFYR paperback edition April 2012
2 4 6 8 10 9 7 5 3 1

The Library of Congress has cataloged the hardcover edition as follows:
Haddix, Margaret Peterson.
Leaving fishers / written by Margaret Peterson Haddix.
p. cm.
Summary: After joining her new friends in the religious group called Fishers of Men, Dorry finds herself immersed in a cult from which she must struggle to extricate herself.
ISBN 978-0-689-81125-8 (hc)
[1. Cults—Fiction. 2. Fanaticism—Fiction. 3. Christian life—Fiction.] I. Title.
PZ7.H1164Le
[Fic]—dc21
96-47857
ISBN 978-1-4424-4314-3 (pbk)
ISBN 978-1-4391-1584-8 (eBook)

For Meredith and Connor

CHAPTER ONE

DORRY WAS EATING ALONE. Again.

She slouched in the hard plastic chair as if that would make her invisible. Which was ridiculous because, of the hundreds of kids crowded into the Crestwood High School cafeteria, not one seemed to care if Dorry was there or on Mars. Three guys in striped polo shirts sat on her right, and two girls in T-shirts sat on her left, but none of them had glanced at Dorry even once since they sat down.

Grimly, Dorry peeled the waxed paper off her peanut-butter-and-cheese sandwich. She took a bite and chewed automatically. Peanut butter and cheese used to be her favorite sandwich, but now it tasted like sadness, like tears held back because she was too proud to cry in front of people she didn't know.

The first week she'd gone around like some robot with a one-message computer chip: "Hi. I'm Dorry Stevens. I'm new." She had grinned fanatically with every greeting, so much that her smile muscles ached by the end of each day. Usually people said "Hi," and then turned back to their friends. Sometimes all she got was a shrug. The worst response had come from a girl in the bathroom that first Friday, a punk-looking girl with triple-pierced ears and an army jacket. Dorry shouldn't have tried, but the girl didn't look like she fit in either.

"Hi. I'm Dorry Stevens. I'm new," Dorry had said hopefully.

The girl looked at her through mascara-clumped eyelashes. "Oh, *God*," she said, and broke out laughing. Then two other girls with heavily pierced ears—one also had a nose ring—came out of the bathroom stalls and laughed with her. Dorry caught a glimpse of her own face in the mirror, her horrified smile frozen like a Halloween mask.

It took every bit of nerve Dorry had not to run straight home—not to the tiny apartment her parents had rented while her father worked in Indianapolis, but the three hundred miles back to Bryden, Ohio, where she'd lived all her life until now. She had plenty of friends there, friends she'd never had to introduce herself to because she'd known most of them practically since she was born.

"Send me home," Dorry begged her parents that

night. "I can live with Denise. Or Donny. Or maybe Marissa's parents won't mind . . ." Denise and Donny were her brother and sister, both about twenty years older than Dorry. Marissa was her best friend.

"Oh, Dorry, you know we can't do that," Dorry's mother said. She didn't add all the reasons they'd hashed out last spring when they found out Dorry's father's factory was closing. He was one of the lucky workers who could transfer to other plants to get their last few years in before retirement. He only had three more years, but that meant Dorry would have to spend her last two years of high school in a strange place. Donny and Denise had actually kind of offered to take Dorry, but they each had three kids and already cramped houses. Dorry's parents kept saying they didn't want to impose on anybody and, besides, what kind of parents would miss their daughter's last two years of high school?

"Mom, this isn't going to work. Nobody likes me, the school's too big—" Dorry stopped because she couldn't go on without crying.

Her mother sighed. "I'm sorry, honey. This is tough on all of us. Give things a little more time. You'll adjust."

But it had been three weeks now, and Dorry hadn't adjusted. She'd given up. She took another bite of her peanut-butter-and-cheese sandwich. The food stuck in her throat, gagging her. If she swallowed again, she was sure she'd choke. And you could bet nobody would bother giving her the Heimlich maneuver. She'd die, and nobody would notice.

"Excuse me. Are you alone? Would you like to eat with us?"

Dorry gulped down the bite of sandwich and looked up at a very pretty blond girl. No matter how much she'd wanted friends before, her first instinct now was denial—*no, I'm just waiting for someone. I don't look pathetic enough to eat alone, do I?* But someone was actually speaking to her. Dorry decided she wouldn't give up after all.

"Sure," she said. "Thanks."

"My friends and I are over there," the girl said, pointing. Dorry couldn't see where she meant in the sea of other kids, but she shoved her sandwich back into her sack, picked up her milk, and stood up.

"I'm Angela Briarstone," the girl said, leading the way.

"Dorry Stevens," Dorry said. She hoped all the people who hadn't noticed her before would see her now, walking and talking with a friend. Well, a potential friend.

"You're new, aren't you?" Angela asked.

Dorry nodded. "We just moved here," she said. "My dad had a job transfer."

Dorry thought that sounded better than explaining about the factory closing down. From what she'd seen and heard at Crestwood, all the kids she'd want to be friends with had parents who were doctors or law-yers or at least presidents of their own companies. And Angela seemed to be one of those kids, judging from the designer labels on her purse and jeans. Dorry's jeans came from K-Mart. But *she* wants *you* to eat with her, Dorry reminded herself.

Angela nodded sympathetically. "That's got to be hard, moving," she said. "Have you had to do a lot of it?"

"What? Oh—no. This is the first time. Before this year, we always lived at home. I mean, back in Bryden. Ohio. And we're going back in three years, so my parents didn't even sell the house. So it's not really like we *moved*, moved. We're just here . . . temporarily."

I've got to shut up, Dorry thought. *Angela's going to think I'm one of those people who only talk about them-selves.* "What about you?" she asked. "Have you always lived here?"

Angela shook her head no, but didn't elaborate, because they had evidently reached her group of friends. She pulled out a chair for Dorry before sitting down in front of her own tray.

"Everybody, this is Dorry," Angela announced. "She just moved here. Dorry, this is Brad, Michael, Jay, Lara, and Kim."

Dorry sat down, nodded, and said "Hi" to each of the others. She was careful not to smile too wide, even though, for the first time in three weeks, she really wanted to. She could have six friends by the end of this lunch and three of them were even boys—cute boys, if you ignored Jay's acne. Of course, they were probably all in couples. Dorry tried to figure out which one was Angela's boyfriend.

"Did you already pray over your meal?" Brad asked. "We were just going to."

"Er—no," Dorry said. "I—"

"Brad, she's going to think you're some kind of religious fanatic," Angela said.

Brad winked at Dorry and bowed his head. "God is great, God is good," he began. "Now it's time to eat this food. Please, God, don't let it kill us."

He looked up, grinning. Dorry thought of her six-year-old nephew Travis, whose most angelic smiles meant he'd just done something like feed his dog blue Kool-Aid so he'd have psychedelic dog droppings.

"Dorry, I ask you—is that the prayer of a religious fanatic?" Brad said.

Dorry turned her head just in time to see Angela giving Brad a slight frown. Something was going on that she didn't understand. "I don't think I know any religious fanatics," Dorry said carefully.

"Really?" Brad said. "No Seventh-Day Adventists? No Mormons? No snake-handling fundamentalists? Where are you from?"

"A small town you've never heard of," Dorry said, a little nervously. She remembered her dad saying, more than once, that you should never talk about religion or politics with people you didn't know.

"Ah, a mystery woman," Brad said in a fake French accent. "She won't reveal her secrets."

Dorry laughed with the others. Brad, she decided, was like Joey Van Camp back in Bryden. Everything was a joke to Joey, and he could make anything sound funny. He was a lot of fun if you remembered never to take him seriously. She decided the religious stuff didn't mean anything to Brad. She relaxed in her chair and started pulling her lunch back out of her sack. Then she looked up and saw Brad grinning at her. He was a lot cuter than Joey Van Camp, she thought, with those blue eyes and straight black hair that fell perfectly across his forehead. Even if it was just a joke, Dorry liked him calling her a mystery woman. Nobody back in Bryden would have even thought of putting her—plain old, dull, dumpy Dorry—in the same sentence as "mystery" or "secrets." Maybe moving wasn't such a bad idea.

"And she still won't talk," Brad announced. "What will it take to get her to crack?"

"I'll take my secrets to the grave," Dorry said, imitating his tone of mock seriousness. She felt foolish and thrilled all at once.

"Oh, but you already told," Angela said, with an odd laugh. "She's from Bryden, Ohio, folks."

Dorry felt a little hurt. Were Brad and Angela dating? Was Angela jealous of him clowning around with Dorry? Brad didn't seem to notice.

"Ah, but you see, that is a mystery, too. Where is this Bryden?" Brad asked. His faux French accent was actually improving.

"Way over in eastern Ohio," Dorry answered. "It's really tiny. Pretty dull place, actually." She got a familiar lump at the back of her throat thinking of Bryden: its tree-lined streets, its stately courthouse, and its four traffic lights, which you could whiz through one after the other if you caught the first one just turning green. Bryden didn't even seem part of the same universe as Crestwood, which was one apartment complex after another by the interstate exit ramps, then rich neighborhoods with security guards and gates farther on. Crestwood didn't have a downtown, just fast-food strips and the mall. And excet for the signs that said, "Welcome to Crestwood" and "Leaving Crestwood," Dorry would have no idea where Crestwood ended and Indianapolis began. All Dorry's friends back in Bryden had been jealous that she was moving to the big city. "You're going to come back so sophisticated we won't know you," Marissa had joked. And, in brave moments, at first Dorry had thought

Crestwood would be exciting. She had imagined hanging out at the mall or going to downtown Indianapolis with friends. Maybe that was still possible.

"So what do you think of Indianapolis?" Angela asked now.

"Um—I guess I like it," Dorry said.

"Such certainty," Brad joked.

"It probably seems overwhelming to you, doesn't it?" Lara said in a quiet voice.

Dorry nodded gratefully. She'd barely noticed Lara when Angela was introducing everyone. Lara had straight brown hair and a plain face. Beside Angela and Kim— both well dressed and carefully made up—Lara faded into the background. But Lara seemed to understand how awful the move had been for Dorry.

Angela gave her a perky smile. "Oh, it's not that bad. You'll fit in in no time."

Dorry wasn't sure what to say to that, so she took another bite of her sandwich and drained her milk carton. She wished the others would keep talking, but they were all grinning at her expectantly. Dorry tried to think of something else to talk about.

"Do people go to the football games around here, or is this the kind of school where no one's big on that?" she asked.

"Oh, none of us are really into football," Angela said. "What about you?"

"Back in Bryden, everyone went to the football games, kindergarten on up. We made it to the state finals last year. Talk about exciting! We filled six buses for the trip to Columbus—" Dorry felt like she was babbling. But it was hard not to when all the others were looking at her and nodding so attentively. *How can it be,* Dorry thought, *that for three weeks nobody knows I exist, and then I suddenly find five people who act like I'm the most fascinating person in the world?*

She went on telling about the state championships: the tied score with three minutes left, the other team's last-minute touchdown, the disappointed Bryden crowd, and the long, sad ride home. "Lots of people said that was the worst moment of their lives," Dorry said.

"I don't mean to interrupt, but I've got to go now," Jay said. "It was very nice meeting you, Dorry."

He stood up. Dorry wondered why he hadn't said anything until now, if he really enjoyed meeting her. Maybe he was shy. Maybe he was just being polite. She smiled back, hoping he really meant it.

"Thanks. You too."

The others began scraping back their chairs and gathering up crumpled napkins and empty milk cartons. The bell was going to ring in a few minutes. Dorry wanted to ask, "Can I eat with you guys tomorrow?" but she thought it would sound too childish, like a little kid on a playground begging, "Let me play with you." All the others had a school lunch, so they had to go to the tray-return window while Dorry walked over to the trash can. She watched Brad and Angela whispering, their heads together. Were they talking about her? Were they making fun of her? She shouldn't have talked so much about the state championship. What other stupid things had she said? Dorry felt lonelier than ever. She dropped her lunch sack into the garbage and turned around.

Suddenly Angela was by her side. "Oh, good, Dorry, I was afraid you might have gotten away. I just wanted to say we'd love to have you eat with us again tomorrow. That is, if you don't have other plans."

"No, I don't. That'd be great," Dorry said.

"Okay!" Angela said, cheerleader peppy. "See you then!"

The bell rang, and Dorry watched her new friends disappear in the rush of kids stampeding out of the cafeteria.

Her new friends. She liked the sound of that.

CHAPTER TWO

DORRY CLIMBED OFF THE bus several steps behind the other four kids who lived in her apartment complex. The bus driver snapped the door shut so fast it almost scraped her leg. She sighed, then started coughing from the heavy exhaust fumes. Six lanes of traffic whizzed behind her. Next door, a power station buzzed behind ominous high gates and warning signs. Electric wires crisscrossed over her head. Ahead, despite the bright September sunshine, the Northview buildings looked as dreary as ever. All the buildings were exactly alike: dull, ugly brown brick, with cheap-looking shutters and poorly fitting doors. Dorry thought her family's door was the only one in the whole complex that shut tight, and that was just because her father had fixed it the very first day. Her mother had set out a ceramic pot of bright yellow chrysanthemums, too,

12

but they had been knocked over and crushed the first night. Her mother didn't bother replacing them.

Dorry watched the other kids race past the Northview complex manager's office. She heard one of them yell a string of expletives, but she wasn't sure if he was mad or just talking. She turned down her street. Out of the corner of her eye, she saw a bright blue sports car turn off the main street into the entrance to the apartment complex. Gleaming in the sunlight, the car slowed, then stopped. Dorry squinted into the sun, watching. Why would someone drive a car like that into a place like Northview? The driver had long blond hair, dark sunglasses, and a purple shirt like Angela had been wearing. Wait a minute. That *was* Angela. Did she live at Northview, too? Were they neighbors?

Dorry turned to wave, imagining in that split second inviting Angela in for some sort of after-school snack— would there be enough chocolate cake left over from dinner last night? Or would Angela be more into Pepsi and potato chips? And beyond that, she could see the two of them becoming really good friends if they lived close. They'd drop by at each other's apartment, do homework together, drive to school together. Dorry would be free of the hated bus. She'd always have a friend around.

The driver of the blue car ducked down out of sight. Dorry's arm froze, mid-wave. Then, embarrassed, she let it fall back to her side. She watched the car. That had been Angela, hadn't it? Maybe she was getting something out of her glove compartment. Maybe she'd dropped a contact. Dorry waited, uncertain, but no blond head reappeared. She took two steps back toward the car, ready to ask Angela if she needed any help. Then she stopped. What if it wasn't Angela? What if it was someone coming to Northview to buy drugs? She'd overheard people talking on the bus. There were drug dealers around.

Dorry turned around, shivering as though she had just barely saved herself from being killed in a drug-war shootout. She hurried on to her family's apartment.

"Dorry? That you?" Her mother called from the bedroom.

Dorry was still blinking at the door, trying once again to adjust to the sight of her family's familiar furniture crammed into the still-unfamiliar apartment. The overstuffed couch, with its pattern of brown and red autumn leaves, just didn't look right without the matching love seat, the scarred end tables on either side, or the pine paneling behind it. But the couch, the coffee table, the recliner, and the TV completely filled the living room. Getting from the front door to the kitchen was like running an obstacle course.

Dorry's mother came out from her bedroom. Her gray pin curls were uncharacteristically mussed, and the left side of her face had strange indentations, like the chenille pattern of her bedspread.

"Mom? Were you sleeping?" Dorry dropped her books on the floor and sank onto the couch.

"No, I just lay down for a few minutes. Don't know why I can't get my get-up-and-go back from this move. Guess it got up and went." Dorry's mother shoved her thick fingers behind her glasses and rubbed her eyes. She sat down in the recliner. "How was school?"

"Okay." Dorry tried to forget about the blue car. She thought about lunch. Afterward, she'd felt as victorious as the Revolutionary War soldiers her boring American History teacher had lectured about in sixth period. *Angela and the others like me*, she told herself over and over. *Of course they like me. They asked me to eat with them tomorrow.*

"I met some new friends," she told her mother. But because of the blue car her voice came out sounding uncertain.

Her mother let her glasses slip back into place on her nose. She peered at Dorry. "I knew you'd make friends soon," she said. "I almost forgot—I got good news today, too. I got a job!"

"Oh, good!" Dorry said. Back in Bryden her mother had worked as a nurse at the county health department. But she'd had trouble finding a job here. "At that nursing home?"

"Yes. I'll have a crazy schedule for a while—lots of evenings, lots of weekends. But I'm hoping that won't last long."

"Good," Dorry said again. If her mother was going to pretend to be happy, she would, too. She'd heard her parents talking about how awful the nursing-home job was. But Dorry knew they needed the money. They hadn't been able to rent out their house back in Bryden because, with the factory closed, there was no one to rent to. And her parents hadn't exactly told her, but she'd figured out that her dad wasn't making as much as he used to. They wouldn't live at Northview Apartments if they didn't have to.

"Between your dad's work schedule and mine, you'll have to be on your own a lot more," Dorry's mother continued. "But we know we can trust you. And you have friends now, so you won't be lonely."

"Uh-huh." Dorry didn't remind her mother they were very, very new friends, not lifelong buddies like Marissa and her other friends back home. Once, years ago, Dorry had overheard her mother telling a neighbor, "You know, I thought I was much too old to deal with another child when Dorry was born. But she slept through the night her first week home from the hospital. She didn't throw a single tantrum as a two-year-old. She's quiet, she cleans up her messes—I don't think there could be an easier child on the face of the earth." From that moment, Dorry had known what her parents expected of her: Don't make trouble. Don't bother us with your problems. And, mostly, she hadn't. But they'd always been there when she needed them. What would it be like if they were both working evening shifts?

"Got a lot of homework?" Dorry's mom asked.

"Uh-huh," Dorry said. "I'll start on it now."

"Come watch Oprah with me when you need a break," Dorry's mom said, reaching for the TV.

Dorry stepped into the kitchen and took the last piece of chocolate cake off the cake plate. It really would have been big enough for two people. She poured a glass of milk and took the food and her books back to her room. It was even more cramped than the living room because she'd refused to leave behind anything from her room back home. Every inch of the walls, ceiling to floor, was covered with posters and pictures. Dorry's eighth-grade graduation photo, with her and Marissa grinning together in matching white gowns, covered the words on the poster of a kitten hanging from a branch by one claw. The ballerina poster she'd gotten in fifth grade leaned into her tacked-up collection of postcards from Florida, Texas, Hawaii, and, now, Bryden, Ohio.

Dorry maneuvered around several teddy bears and flopped across the bed. She took a bite of cake and opened her Algebra II book. From the living room, she could hear the crowd applauding Oprah. She opened her notebook to a fresh sheet of paper, but couldn't concentrate long enough to write the number of the first problem.

She began doodling. The pencil spun out circles, and, on top of the circles, the outline of a car. A sports car. What if it had been Angela in the blue car? What if she'd ducked because she didn't want Dorry to see her?

CHAPTER THREE

DORRY WAS STILL TRYING to forget the blue car when Brad waved her over to a table near the wall at lunch the next day. "We saved you a seat," he told her. "It's just like heaven—your place is reserved if you but ask for it."

Dorry felt a thrill of relief that they'd remembered her. But what did heaven have to do with anything? Angela was frowning at Brad again. Did he just like to joke about religion? Dorry told herself it didn't matter, either way. Back in Bryden, her family had gone to the Bryden Methodist Church sometimes—Christmas and Easter, mainly. As soon as they got in the car afterward, Dorry's mom always pulled her feet out of her tight heels and rubbed her bunions, while Dorry's dad shucked off his tie and said, "That's enough religion for me for a while. They pay that guy just to talk one hour a week—wouldn't you think he'd have something more interesting to say?"

Now Angela smiled at Dorry and asked, "Are you having a good day?"

"Not too bad," Dorry said, even though it had been. "I had a really hard pop quiz in American Lit."

"Let me guess—Mrs. Crenshaw and *The Scarlet Letter*?" Brad said.

"Yeah." Dorry hesitated, too ashamed to say she thought she might have flunked the quiz. Back in Bryden, she'd never gotten anything but As and Bs, and her counselor had called her "definite college material." No one here seemed to think that.

"I could help you if you're having trouble," Lara said.

Dorry turned eagerly to Lara. "Really?"

"Lara did really well in that class," Angela said. "You should let her help. She likes explaining things."

"Is after school Friday soon enough?" Lara asked. "Mrs. Crenshaw usually only gives quizzes once a week."

"That's great," Dorry said. "Except—I can't miss my bus."

"I can drive you home," Lara said.

Dorry saw her opportunity. "I live at Northview Apartments," she said almost defiantly. She looked over at Angela, wanting her to say, "Oh, so do I!" or, "I was just there yesterday . . ." Angela's expression didn't change. She brought a forkful of salad to her mouth. Then she bent over to get a sip of milk. Her hair fell forward, hiding her face.

"I'm not sure I know how to get there," Lara said. "But it doesn't matter. You can show me."

"Okay," Dorry said, embarrassed. She bit into her sandwich. If it hadn't been Angela in the blue car yesterday, Dorry was on the verge of making a fool of herself. How could she have thought Angela might live at Northview? Angela had on an expensive-looking sweater and earrings that were probably real diamonds. And she wanted to be Dorry's friend. Dorry shouldn't screw that up.

Dorry ate with her new friends every day after that. It wasn't always the same people—Brad and Angela were always there, but Lara, Kim, Michael, and Jay rotated in and out. Dorry started running into her friends in the halls between classes, too. Angela's psychology class met around the corner from Dorry's history class, and she began waiting outside the door afterward for Dorry. Brad popped up at the oddest moments, usually yelling through the halls, "Are we still on for lunch?"

Dorry always hoped everyone in the crowded hall overheard. Sometimes other girls gave her odd looks, and Dorry had to stop herself from laughing out loud. Could these city girls be jealous?

By Friday, Dorry had practically forgotten that she'd felt lonely and friendless only four days earlier. It was that afternoon that Lara helped her study *The Scarlet Letter*. Lara drove her to Burger King, treated her to fries and a milk shake, and patiently went through the book chapter by chapter until Dorry could discuss Hester Prynne's sin and redemption almost as nimbly as Lara did.

"Thanks to you, maybe I'll be able to get a good enough grade to go to college after all," Dorry said, only half joking, as they finished. "You've saved my life."

Lara didn't smile back. She leaned forward, forehead wrinkled. "Speaking of salvation . . . You're using the right words, but do you really believe any of this?" she asked.

Dorry took the straw out of her almost-empty milk shake cup and began playing with it. "What do you mean? Do I believe the book? It's fiction, right?"

Lara's steady gaze made Dorry uncomfortable. She pretended to look for another French fry, though she knew they were all gone.

"No, no. Forget *The Scarlet Letter*. I mean, do you believe in God? Do you believe that sin separates us from God?" Lara leaned in closer with each word.

Dorry looked around. A group of teenaged boys was only three tables away. "I guess," Dorry answered. "I mean, I haven't really thought about it much, but I guess I believe in God."

"I didn't used to." Lara sat back, suddenly acting almost relaxed. "It's strange, but last year when I was writing all those right answers on Mrs. Crenshaw's tests, I was an atheist."

"Really?" Dorry was fascinated. She'd never known an atheist before. "Why? Didn't your parents and everybody tell you what you were supposed to believe?"

"Oh, they didn't care. It's not like *they* really believe in anything. But they didn't like the other things I was doing."

Dorry waited, torn between wanting to know the rest of Lara's story and fearing Lara would tell it. What if it was really awful?

"My parents got divorced when I was twelve," Lara said. "I'm not proud of this, but after that I was really promiscuous. I slept with anyone who wanted me, and lots of guys did because, you know, I *would*."

"At twelve?" Dorry said. She wasn't sure, but she thought she was still playing with dolls then.

"Twelve, thirteen, fourteen, yeah. I thought I was so grown up. A lot of the guys treated me badly, and I figured, that's life. I thought, what's it matter? It didn't make any sense to me that there would be a God, because everything was so bad."

"But—" Dorry wanted to argue, but she didn't know what to say.

Lara held up her hand. "That was then, not now. I was *so* screwed up."

"So what happened?"

Lara bit her lip. "Has anyone told you about Pastor Jim and the Fishers of Men?"

Dorry shook her head. She was about to joke that it sounded like one of those old pop groups her parents talked about—Bill Haley and the Comets, Pastor Jim and the Fishers of Men. But Lara looked so intense Dorry didn't dare say anything. She leaned her milk shake cup back and let the last drops run down her throat.

"It's, well, Fishers of Men is a religious group, of course, and Pastor Jim is the leader," Lara said. "But he's not like other ministers, and Fishers isn't like any church I've ever heard of. All our friends are Fishers."

The milk shake went down the wrong way and Dorry began coughing. "Brad? Angela? Jay?" she said as soon as she could.

"Yeah. Yeah." Lara nodded rapidly. "Everyone."

Dorry began flipping the straw between her fingers again. She remembered Brad's religious comments and jokes. So that was it. He was some sort of religious fanatic. But she remembered him making fun of fanatics that first day, Monday. And no one had tried to convert her or anything. Wasn't that what a fanatic would do?

"I can tell what you're thinking," Lara said quietly. "You mention religion nowadays, and people think about cults. But Fishers isn't like that. It's the answer to everything."

Dorry kept quiet. *They're not going to like me anymore,* she thought. *As soon as they find out I'm just a plain old Methodist, and I can't be a Fisher, they're not going to like me.*

"Do you mind if I tell you about Fishers?" Lara asked.

Dorry shrugged, curious in spite of herself.

"Believe me, you couldn't find anyone more skeptical than I was about religion," Lara said. "But then one day last spring, I was walking out of school and I bumped into this guy. I hit him so hard we both almost fell down. It was Pastor Jim, though I didn't know it then. He was really nice about everything. I told him I was sorry, and he said, 'That's okay. God can forgive all your sins.'"

"And that made you stop being an atheist?" Dorry couldn't believe it.

"Not just like that. But it got me thinking. I had felt so ashamed of myself for so long, I couldn't even remember what it was like not to feel guilty. But then, to have Pastor Jim say that to me, in that big, sonorous voice he has—you'll hear him. You'll see. I started wondering if I could start over, not have that guilt following me around. But I didn't know what to do. I didn't know who Pastor Jim was, or where to find him. So I started hanging around out front at school, looking for him before and after school. I started telling guys no, because I was too busy looking for Pastor Jim. Then one day, there he was, talking to someone over by the parking lot. I ran the length of the sidewalk to get to him and tugged on his coat—kind of like Mary Magdalene with Jesus in the Bible. I said, 'You don't remember me, but you told me my sins could be forgiven. Now I want to know. How?'"

"What did he say?" Dorry asked.

"He told me that Jesus died for me, that He took the punishment for my sins so I could go free."

"You'd never heard of Jesus before?" Dorry was a little disappointed. She'd expected something more dramatic than the same old stuff she'd heard at church.

"Of course I'd heard of Jesus," Lara said. "But I thought He was just a legend. A fairy tale that weak, stupid people made up to justify being narrow-minded."

"And just like that, Pastor Jim made you change your mind?" Dorry tried not to sound too skeptical. Back in Bryden, just about everybody went to church, but the only people who went around talking about sin and Jesus and salvation were the Holy Rollers, the ones who went to the Church of the Savior's Blood. Everyone knew they were weird. Dorry had heard that they spoke in tongues and ran up and down the aisles in the middle of the service if they felt like it.

Dorry knew she was looking at Lara the way she might look at one of the Holy Rollers. But Lara didn't seem to mind. She looked happier than Dorry had probably looked in her entire life. She practically glowed. It reminded Dorry of hokey science-fiction movies where people started glowing and then aliens beamed them up into space.

"It wasn't so much what Pastor Jim said, as the way he said it," Lara said. "He seemed so . . . calm, so at peace with himself and his beliefs. He touched my hand and said, 'Your sins are forgiven,' and I felt a power jolting through me, and it was like, for the first time in my life, I could see the truth. I felt the Holy Spirit."

"Oh," Dorry said.

Lara laughed. "You're not exactly thrilled by my story, are you?"

"It's not that," Dorry protested. "I mean, I guess I'm happy for you that you have your, uh, beliefs—"

"But you feel a little left out, that you've never had a similar experience, that God's never spoken to you so profoundly?"

On her own, Dorry would never have said that was the source of her discomfort. But she found herself saying, "Yes." And maybe Lara was right, maybe that was it.

"So will you come to a Fishers of Men get-together with me tonight?"

Dorry blinked, not sure how they'd gotten from Lara's story to this invitation.

"It's a no-pressure situation," Lara said. "You go, you don't like it, that's it, we forget about it."

"And nobody's mad at me?" Dorry asked, thinking of eating alone again.

"Nobody's mad at you. No big deal. But if you do like it—just think what you might gain."

Dorry couldn't think of anything—she wasn't a Holy Roller, she couldn't imagine having a Holy Spirit jolt or glowing the way Lara did. But she knew she couldn't tell Lara that. And it wasn't as if she had any other plans. Both her parents had to work evening shifts. She had expected to just stay home alone with the TV.

"Okay," she said.

CHAPTER FOUR

IT WAS A PARTY.

Walking in behind Lara, Dorry saw balloons and bright lights and a crowd. She remembered something her friend Marissa had said before she left Bryden: "You'll have to tell us everything about your first party in the big city."

"I bet it's not in a barn," Dorry had joked, because her going-away party was. It was a cleaned-up barn that Marissa's uncle rented out for wedding receptions and 4-H dinners and other events, but if you breathed in really deeply you could still catch the faintest whiff of the hogs that had originally lived there. Then Dorry had felt bad, because Marissa had looked so hurt. "And I'm sure it won't be as much fun," Dorry added quickly. "I'll miss you."

Now Dorry did miss Marissa, and the safety of having someone she knew would hang out with her the whole night. She wasn't entirely sure what Lara would do. But it was exciting to be somewhere new, to hear pulsating rock music (so much hipper than the country tunes that dominated at Bryden parties), to catch a glimpse of Brad and Michael across the room and think, *Maybe they'll talk to me more here, away from school.* The party was in the clubhouse of an apartment complex halfway across Indianapolis from Crestwood. That struck Dorry as very grown up. And it was a much nicer apartment complex than Northview. Dorry could see an indoor swimming pool through the row of sliding-glass doors along the far wall.

"Not too scary yet, is it?" Lara asked, leaning her head close to Dorry's to be heard over the music.

"No," Dorry said, though her stomach was doing flip-flops. Sure, it looked like a perfectly normal, fun party, but what if everyone started acting weird and religious? What would Dorry do then?

"Who are all these people?" she asked. "They don't all go to Crestwood, do they?"

"No," Lara said. "They're from schools all over the city. Some are from the colleges around here, too."

Wow, Dorry thought. A party with college kids. She looked around, trying to figure out who was in college, who was in high school. But no one stood out. There were at least fifty people in the clubhouse. Several kids were out in the middle dancing. Another group stood back by what appeared to be a refreshments table. Others were clustered in groups of threes and fours all around the room.

"Come on," Lara said. "Let's go say hi to people."

They circled around the dance floor. Angela was out there, dancing across from a tall, dark-haired guy. She danced just the way Dorry would have expected, with a smooth grace that almost looked dignified. Her long hair floated around her shoulders, bouncing with the beat. She turned toward Dorry. Dorry grinned and gave a little wave. For a split second something ugly crossed Angela's face—if Dorry hadn't known better, she would have sworn that Angela was furious at the very sight of her. But that was gone in a flash, and Angela gave her a huge smile. She mouthed words that looked like, "Talk to you later," and made a face and a helpless gesture at her dance partner. The whole pantomime lasted no longer than the angry look, but it left Dorry feeling that Angela was delighted to see her after all, that she'd rather talk to Dorry than dance.

Dorry followed Lara to a group that included Jay and Kim, the quietest of the lunch gang.

"I talked Dorry into coming," Lara announced.

"Great," Jay said. "I didn't realize . . . are you having fun?"

"Sure," Dorry said. "I was so happy to be invited."

There was an awkward pause, then Lara introduced Dorry to the others standing with them, Jenny and Tom. But she barely had a chance to say hi before Angela and Brad were beside them.

"Dorry!" Angela exclaimed. "What a great surprise!"

She hugged Dorry. Dorry could smell the herbal shampoo in Angela's hair. Then Angela let go.

"Lara asked me to come," Dorry said. "She told me a little about Fishers of Men."

She tried to keep her voice steady, but the "Fishers of Men" part came out like a question. Dorry longed to ask, "Why didn't you tell me about Fishers of Men?" or, "Why didn't you invite me to this party?" or, "Will you still be my friend if I'm not in your group?" But she knew better than to say anything like that. She looked down.

"Ah," Brad said in a bantering tone. "Our little secret is out."

Dorry looked up in time to catch his devilish grin.

Angela laughed lightly. "It's hardly a secret. Everyone at Crestwood knows we're in Fishers. I thought you knew about it, too."

"No," Dorry said. "I'm new, remember?" She didn't like the way she sounded—whiny and wronged, like a little kid who hadn't gotten her way.

"I'm really sorry," Angela said. "I was going to talk to

you about Fishers soon, but I didn't want to, you know, scare you off or make you feel like I was pressuring you to join. And I wanted to invite you to this party, but since it was a Fishers event, I thought it might be better to wait. We have parties all the time."

For a suspicious moment, Dorry thought Angela had caught herself in a lie. First she said she thought Dorry knew about Fishers, then she said she had planned to tell her about it later. Dorry thought of the way her father talked back to political commercials on TV: "Now, wait just a cotton-picking minute. It can't be both ways at once." But Angela had her arm around Dorry's shoulder again. She was smiling kindly, not like a liar, but like a friend. Dorry suddenly saw how both things could be true, that Angela thought Dorry knew something about Fishers, but that Angela planned eventually to tell her more—an in-depth confidence, the kind shared between friends.

"Anyhow," Angela said. "You're here now. And that's great. Are you hungry? There's lots of food." Brad and Angela ushered Dorry over to the refreshments table, which was loaded with chips and deli trays and two-liter bottles of pop.

"A feast fit for a king," Brad said. "Or queen or princess in this case."

Dorry giggled, because it was impossible not to laugh

at Brad's goofy expression. And she suddenly felt light and giddy. She was at a party in Indianapolis, in a fancy clubhouse with an indoor pool. She was with friends, good-looking, interesting, nice friends who really cared about her. If only Marissa and everyone else back in Bryden could see her now.

Brad handed Dorry a paper plate, and she started filling it. When they reached the end of the table, the three of them stood off to the side eating—or, in Angela's case, sipping a diet Coke. Someone turned down the music, so it was easier to talk now.

"So did Lara get you straightened out on your American Lit?" Angela asked.

"Yes," Dorry said. "She was a lot of help."

"Good," Angela said. "You do really well in school, don't you? Tell Brad about your history test."

Dorry felt honored that Angela remembered. She'd only mentioned it in passing in the hallway.

"I'm all ears," Brad said, and somehow managed to wiggle both of them at once.

"How do you do that?" Dorry asked.

"Great muscle control," he said. "But what about history?"

"Oh, it really wasn't anything," Dorry said, trying not to sound like she was bragging. "I just got an A on a test I was really scared about. I've been worried about my grades because Crestwood is bigger than Bryden and the teachers expect so much more. . . ."

"But if you're smart, you're smart. No matter what school you're at," Angela said.

"Right," Brad said. "And you are smart."

They flashed her twin, caring smiles. Dorry took a step back. She'd never had friends like these, who seemed to think so much of her. It made her a little uncomfortable. She missed the mocking "Get over yourself" Marissa always tossed out whenever Dorry had fretted about grades back in Bryden.

"It's just that I want to go to college, and I'll have to get a scholarship, so—" Dorry jumped as a hand firmly grasped her shoulder.

"Don't tell me," a voice boomed behind her. "This is Dorry."

Dorry turned. From the voice she expected to see a giant bear of a man, someone like Paul Bunyan in the folktales her teacher had read to her class back in fifth grade. But the man behind her was only a little taller than she was, five-eight or so, and slender. He had thick, stylishly cut brown hair and a neat mustache. His eyes were a strange, piercing green. He clearly wasn't a high school or college student, but Dorry thought he wasn't much older.

"I'm Pastor Jim," he said, in a slightly lower voice.

"Brad and Angela and the others have told me how much they've enjoyed getting to know you." He squeezed her shoulder in a friendly way and dropped his arm.

"Uh, thanks," Dorry said. "I like them, too."

Pastor Jim laughed, and his laugh matched his voice—booming and rich. Dorry wasn't sure what she'd expected from Lara's story, but this man was too handsome and too young. Dorry thought about what he'd said to Lara the first time they met. She braced herself for him to say something about sin or forgiveness. She tried to think how to answer. How about, "Don't worry. I'm a Methodist, not an atheist"?

"Are you enjoying yourself?" he asked.

"Yes," Dorry said.

"Fishers of Men throw great parties," he said. "I hope you'll come to lots more."

Somehow the way he said it made the simple words seem vastly significant. He seemed overcome with joy at Dorry's presence, overwhelmingly eager to see her come back.

Then someone at the other end of the room shouted, "Pastor Jim," and he excused himself with a parting wink and a final squeeze of Dorry's shoulder. Dorry watched him leave, thinking how different he was from Reverend Patton back at the Methodist Church in Bryden. Reverend Patton was probably sixty, a squat, balding man you'd never notice in a crowded room. He spoke in a barely audible monotone. Dorry had heard her sister Denise and sister-in-law Charlene joke that they'd like to hire Reverend Patton to put their kids to sleep at night: "Just a short bedtime prayer from him and they'd be out all night," Denise had said last Easter.

Pastor Jim would be better at morning wakeup calls. There was something about him—something more than good looks, more than the booming voice. Dorry couldn't have adequately described it if her life depended on it. He had a presence, an aura almost, that affected everyone around him. Angela and Brad were beaming.

"He's incredible, isn't he?" Angela breathed.

"My hero," Brad said. For once, Dorry thought, he wasn't joking.

Dorry shifted uncomfortably, feeling out of place. She wasn't a Fisher, after all. Her tennis shoes squeaked on the tile floor. Brad and Angela snapped their attention back to her. "What were we talking about? Your grades?" Angela asked.

"Yeah, but never mind," Dorry said. "Can you tell me about Fishers? I mean, I really don't know anything about it except that it's a religious group and you're all in it."

"Sure," Angela said. She had a jubilant gleam in her eye. "I don't know about you, but I was always turned off by religion. My family's Episcopalian—talk about boring. Fishers isn't like that. We really try to live by the Word, and to revel in the joy and excitement of being God's children."

"She just learned that word today," Brad said. "From a vocabulary list in English. 'Revel.' Not exactly an Angela word, is it?"

"Oh, stop." Angela laughed. "You try describing it."

"Life is good in Fishers," Brad said. "It's like the Bible says: If God is for you, who can be against you? What's there to be unhappy about if you're right with God?"

Dorry thought about that. All her new friends did seem incredibly happy, incredibly satisfied. She'd been eating lunch with them for a week, and had never once heard anyone complain, even jokingly. And they all seemed so sure of themselves—Dorry couldn't imagine any of her friends back in Bryden walking up to a total stranger and inviting them to lunch, the way Angela had with Dorry. Dorry had thought before that Angela was just more confident and sophisticated because she was from a big city. But maybe it was because of Fishers.

"You're welcome to come to our service on Sunday," Angela said. "I could take you."

"Um, okay," Dorry said. She and her parents hadn't

gone to church at all in Indianapolis, and she really hadn't missed it. But she was curious now.

"Great," Angela replied.

Dorry feared more religion talk, but after that they talked about a prank someone had played at school, painting a huge rock outside the door with the school colors of Crestwood's arch rival. Before long, Angela excused herself to go to the bathroom. Dorry marveled at her luck, being alone with Brad. But suddenly Kim and Jay and Michael were there, too.

"You need to—" Jay started to say to Brad, but broke off when he saw Dorry listening. He cleared his throat and began again. "Sorry, kids, the party's breaking up. And Brad here is on cleanup duty." Then he added, just to Dorry, "We only have the clubhouse rented for three hours."

"Oh." Dorry realized she hadn't seen Lara since the very beginning of the party. She hadn't left, had she? Dorry let herself drift into fantasy for a second. Maybe Brad or Michael would have to take her home. She imagined a quiet car, intimate talk. But then they'd have to see that she lived in awful Northview.

"Excuse me," she said, thinking she ought to look for Lara.

"Going to the bathroom?" Kim asked. "I'll show you where it is."

Figuring she might as well start looking there, Dorry followed Kim through the crowd, out of the main room and down a hallway, past the manager's office. Dorry didn't see Lara anywhere.

"Here it is," Kim said. "Want to go first?"

"No, that's okay. You can," Dorry said.

Kim went inside and locked the door. Dorry felt like a fool standing around outside the bathroom, so she wandered on down the hall to see what the rest of the clubhouse looked like. She passed a water fountain and a wall full of tasteful art. She was about to turn back when she heard voices around the corner.

"—was mine! You knew that! You're a thief, that's what you are!"

Was that Angela? Dorry listened intently. The reply was muffled. "—wasn't like that. I just thought, why wait? She needs it—"

It was Lara, earnest and pleading. They were fighting about something. Dorry wanted to listen, but she didn't want them to come out and see her. They'd think she was eavesdropping. She *was* eavesdropping.

"Dorry?" Kim called from behind. Guiltily, Dorry turned around. She rushed back to the bathroom. "Your turn," Kim said.

Dorry tried to act normal, but Kim gave her a puzzled look. Dorry went into the bathroom. When she came out,

40

Lara and Angela were standing with Kim. They were all smiling, acting normal.

"There you are, Dorry." Lara said. "Having fun? I forgot—I have to help clean up. Is it okay if Angela takes you home?"

Dorry looked from Lara to Angela. Were they still mad at each other? They couldn't be—they were leaning together toward Dorry, both obviously wanting her to agree. "That's fine," Dorry said.

"I've just got to borrow Brad's car," Angela said. "I'll be right back."

"Why Brad's car?" Dorry asked. "If it's a problem, I can wait for Lara. My parents won't be home yet, anyway—"

"No, there's no problem," Angela said, waving her hand airily. "It's just, oh, complicated logistics." She disappeared down the hall. Dorry walked more slowly with Kim and Lara toward the main door of the clubhouse.

"Did you meet Pastor Jim?" Lara asked. "Isn't he great?"

Dorry nodded. "He was very nice," she said, though "nice" was hardly the right word.

"Just wait until you hear him preach," Kim said. "You forget you're in church."

In a few minutes, Angela came back, waving keys. "Ready?" she asked Dorry. "Bye, Kim. Bye, Lara. See you Sunday."

Angela hustled Dorry out the door and to the car, chattering about the party, Brad's car, the weather. Angela expertly pulled out of a tight parking space and drove out of the apartment complex. They were in the thick of traffic on Meridian before Dorry realized she hadn't had a chance to say good-bye to all her friends.

CHAPTER FIVE

ANGELA'S CHATTER ENDED IN the car. She drove for dozens of blocks in silence. Dorry thought ruefully about her fantasy of Brad or one of the other guys taking her home. Right car, wrong driver.

"Everybody likes you. You know that, don't you?" Angela said suddenly. She stopped at a traffic light and flashed a dazzling smile at Dorry.

"Well, sure. I guess so," Dorry said. She turned toward the window to hide an embarrassed grin.

"We feel so lucky to have gotten to know you," Angela said. "If I hadn't seen you sitting by yourself on Monday . . . think what we would have missed."

"Uh-huh," Dorry said. She wasn't sure what to say. Kids didn't talk like that back in Bryden. But Angela was still talking.

"I wasn't sure . . . Sometimes people don't tell others what they mean to them. That's something I've learned in Fishers. You've got to let people know how important they are. And you are important."

Dorry felt even more flattered, and more uncomfortable. Should she tell Angela she liked her, too?

"There's something else . . . This is a little embarrassing, but I don't want you to be confused by anything." Angela paused. The light changed. She turned onto a cloverleaf entrance ramp for 465. Dorry waited, suddenly unsure where the conversation was headed.

"Kim said at the end of the party, when you were waiting for the bathroom, you might have overheard Lara and me talking," Angela said finally, glancing away from the curving road to watch Dorry.

Dorry gulped. "I'm sorry. I didn't mean to—I just—"

Angela waved away Dorry's apologies. "Oh, nobody's blaming you. It's not *your* fault." Angela made it sound like someone else deserved blame, and plenty of it, but she was too kind to say so. Dorry was just relieved Angela wasn't mad at her.

Angela accelerated, pulling out onto the freeway. "The only reason I bring it up is that . . . I was thinking about what we said," she continued. "And depending on what you heard, you could misunderstand. . . . What exactly did you hear?"

"You . . . called Lara a thief," Dorry said hesitantly. She was glad it was darker inside the car now and Angela couldn't see her face. "Did she take something of yours? Then I heard her say something like, 'It wasn't like that. She needed it as soon as possible.'"

Angela didn't even try to look at Dorry now. She peered intently at the traffic around her, changing lanes with a practiced air. "And that's all you heard?"

"Yes," Dorry said. "It's none of my business. I'll forget I heard anything." Of course, she couldn't forget. Already, she was thinking of Lara differently. And Angela, too. Maybe these Fishers people weren't so perfect after all. She looked out the window, just wishing she were home and didn't have to discuss this with Angela. It was the first time she'd ever longed to be at Northview.

"No," Angela said. "You deserve an explanation. Lara has a problem. Kleptomania, I guess it's called. You've heard about people who can't stop taking things, whether they really want them or not? We thought Lara had overcome it since she joined Fishers. I don't think she'd stolen anything in months. But then at the party, I saw her take my necklace out of my purse. She did it right in front of me, like she wanted me to see. It was a cry for help."

Dorry frowned doubtfully, though she couldn't think of any reason that Angela would lie. When had Lara had time to take Angela's necklace? Angela had been with

Dorry practically the whole time. But Angela had left to go to the bathroom. Maybe it had happened then.

"I don't understand. Why was your necklace in your purse?" Dorry asked, then worried that Angela would take the question the wrong way. Dorry didn't want Angela to think she didn't believe her.

"The clasp broke," Angela said. She evidently didn't mind questions. "I didn't want to lose it. Look, I wouldn't have told you about Lara, except I thought it would be worse not to. I hope this doesn't make you think badly of her. She really needs our friendship. We—the Fishers—have been trying to help her."

Angela said "our friendship," casually, and that made the phrase sound even more wonderful to Dorry. She liked it that Angela was treating her as a partner, someone who would help take care of Lara. She liked the thought that Lara needed help from her, Dorry.

Angela glanced at Dorry again. "This is all a little . . . embarrassing for Lara. You won't tell anyone else, will you?"

"Of course not," Dorry said.

"I knew we could count on you," Angela said.

Angela pulled off 465 and Dorry began directing her to Northview. Dorry was glad it was dark and Angela couldn't see much of the complex. They pulled up in front of Dorry's apartment.

"Thanks so much for coming," Angela said, as if she

herself had invited Dorry to the party. "About Sunday morning—I'll pick you up for the service at eight thirty. You'll love it. I promise."

"Okay," Dorry said. "Thanks. Bye."

Dorry got out of the car and waved as Angela pulled out. Angela gestured that she would wait for Dorry to go inside. Dorry turned around. She was surprised by how much light leaked out from around the edges of the curtains on the apartment windows—surely she'd only left one lamp on. She unlocked the door and pushed it open.

"Dorry! Where have you been?" Her mother grabbed Dorry and hugged her tight. "We thought something awful had happened. . . ." Her mother pushed Dorry back and looked into her face. "How could you do this to us?"

As if too weak with relief to keep standing, Dorry's mother collapsed onto the couch, pulling Dorry down with her. Dorry's father was there, too. His eyes were cold and hard in his deeply lined face. Dorry knew that look of barely restrained fury—it had accompanied every single one of her childhood spankings.

"I—I was just at a party with my friends," Dorry said, stumbling over the words, even though she knew that made her sound guilty. "I thought you both had to work until midnight."

"So you thought it was okay to run around wild?" Dorry's dad asked.

Dorry was still caught in her mother's embrace. She pulled away and sat on the edge of the coffee table. "No, no, it wasn't like that. This was a church group I was with." The word "church" had a magical effect, softening both of their faces. But they still looked mad. Dorry rushed to explain. "I would have left a note, but I thought I'd be home before either of you—"

"You should have called me at work and told me where you were going. Asked permission," Dorry's mom said.

"I never did that back home in Bryden," Dorry said.

"This isn't Bryden," Dorry's dad said.

A week earlier, that would have been a cue for Dorry to plead, "Then send me back there." But now she only sat still, in stony silence. Just when she'd had a good time at the party, when Angela had told her everybody liked her and even asked for her help with Lara—why did her parents have to ruin everything?

Dorry's mother patted Dorry's knee. "I guess everything's all right now. You didn't do anything wrong. We're just bound to worry, here in the city, since you hear about all the crime around here. But if you were with some church group . . ."

Dorry looked at her father. "Dad?"

"I reckon your mother's right. But you call her the next time, you hear?" he said grudgingly.

"Okay," Dorry said.

Her father got up and walked to the window. He moved aside the curtain and looked out at the bleak parking lot. "I didn't want to move here either," he said. "But we did and that's that. It's only for three years."

Dorry started to answer, to say she hadn't complained. Not this time. Then she decided he was saying that for her mother's benefit.

Her father dropped the curtain. "I'd better call work." He brushed past Dorry to the phone in the kitchen.

Dorry looked inquisitively at her mother. "Why *are* you both home?"

"I wasn't feeling too good so they sent me home early. When I got here and you weren't home I called your dad. We were going to call the police if you weren't back by ten thirty."

"The police!" Dorry was horrified.

"Yeah. I would have called them right away, but I figured they'd just think we were a couple of hysterical hicks. Don't worry us like this again, okay?"

"Okay." Dorry sat down next to her mother on the couch. "Do you still feel sick?"

"I was so upset about you, I kind of forgot about it. But yeah, basically, I feel like I've been run over by a Mack truck. Don't know what's wrong with me."

Dorry's dad hung up the phone. "Well, I've still got a job, but they want me in for the six a.m. shift to make up for this. I'm going to bed."

49

"You should go, too, Mom," Dorry said. "Get some rest. You'll feel better tomorrow."

"Hope so," her mother said, heaving herself up from the couch.

When both of Dorry's parents had disappeared into their bedroom and shut the door, she relaxed and leaned her head back against the couch. She felt like she'd stepped off a roller coaster. Her parents' anger had been like an unexpected plunge at the end, when she'd thought the ride was over.

Dorry replayed everything in her mind, starting with the trip to Burger King with Lara. That seemed so long ago now. Dorry slid lower on the couch. She remembered laughing and talking with Brad and Angela, meeting Pastor Jim, hearing Angela say, "Everybody likes you. You know that, don't you?" She frowned, thinking of the fight she'd heard between Angela and Lara. Except it wasn't really a fight if it was for Lara's own good. So Lara was a kleptomaniac. What had she meant by ". . . she needs it"? Who would need a broken necklace? Angela hadn't explained that part. Maybe she couldn't. If Lara was a kleptomaniac, her reasoning wouldn't make sense.

Dorry slid down sideways, stretching her legs out on the couch. She could be a little crazy, herself. Before Angela had explained about Lara's problem, Dorry had almost suspected they were fighting about her.

CHAPTER SIX

DORRY GOT UP EARLY Sunday morning and pulled on her nicest outfit, a flowered jumper and matching shirt that looked like silk if you didn't get too close. She tried to forget that the material of the dress pulled too tightly across her midsection. She put on lip gloss without glancing in the mirror. She knew it would only deliver bad news. Her skin had been breaking out something awful since they'd moved, and her hair had never been anything but uncontrollable. Back home, Marissa had gone through a phase where she'd wanted to become a beautician, and she'd taken on Dorry's hair as her personal mission.

"It's not a bad color—really, brown's okay, and it is thick. Maybe one of those new shags would help," Marissa had said.

So Dorry had been crazy enough to follow her advice,

and the haircut had looked awful from the beginning. Now she ran a comb through her hair as usual, without much hope that it would help.

By eight fifteen, Dorry was sitting by the window pulling on her shoes. Both of her parents were sleeping late, and she wanted to make sure Angela didn't wake them knocking at the door or ringing the bell. She looked out at the Northview parking lot and wondered what the Fishers service would be like. Probably boring like Bryden Methodist, she decided. She'd have to figure out how to get everyone to stay friends with her without having to go to church.

A rusty yellow car pulled in and parked at the far end. Dorry knew that wasn't Angela. Then she remembered she didn't know what Angela's car looked like. Surely she wouldn't have Brad's again. Dorry's stomach began doing flip-flops. She chewed a ragged hangnail on her right thumb. Since Friday she'd been trying to focus just on the good things about her new friends. But if Angela was driving a bright blue sports car, that would mean she'd been at Northview on Monday, and had avoided Dorry. Then Dorry would have to ask her about it, or always wonder. And how could they be friends then?

Angela showed up at eight twenty-six, in a dark blue Mercedes.

Relief washed over Dorry, then awe—*I have a friend*

who drives a Mercedes? She grabbed her purse and rushed out the door.

Angela was getting out of the car, stepping gingerly in her high heels on the cracked, weedy blacktop of the parking lot.

"I'm sorry," Dorry said. "My family's not really this poor. It's just that my parents still have to pay taxes and stuff on our house back home, and—"

Angela held up her hand like a stop sign. "Don't worry about it. I don't choose my friends based on money. Think about it—Jesus Himself never even owned a house. Like all Fishers, I live by His example." She circled the Mercedes and held open the passenger door. Dorry got in. Angela stood close, holding the door.

"So it's not an issue, all right?" she said.

"All right," Dorry replied.

"Good." Angela shut the door.

The Mercedes rode smoothly and quietly. Dorry never felt the Northview speed bumps. She never heard the traffic or the hum of the electric station next door.

"The service actually isn't until nine thirty, but the music starts at nine and it's so inspiring, no one wants to miss that," Angela was saying.

"Where is the church, anyway?" Dorry asked.

Angela shook her head. "*We* are the church. There's no building. We follow Christ's example in that—He never built a church. The last couple months we've just rented the Durstin Auditorium downtown."

Even Dorry had heard of that. It was big. They had rock concerts there. "How many people are in Fishers?"

"Several hundred," Angela said. "Maybe a thousand. I don't know. Numbers aren't important. It's what's in people's hearts. It's the spirit we generate together . . . You'll see."

When they got to the auditorium, Dorry could hear the music from the sidewalk. They pushed through giant doors to a huge room where row upon row of people— old, young, white, black, some in dresses or suits, others in jeans and T-shirts—were standing or swaying by their seats.

And everybody, *everybody* was singing.

"Rejoice in the Lord always, and again I say rejoice," some girls trilled, and then male voices picked up the refrain while the girls sang, "Rejoice, rejoice, again I say rejoice." It was a round. Dorry remembered singing rounds in school. But she'd never been overwhelmed by the sound and the echo, as she was now. Caught in the swirl of music, one "rejoice" chasing the other, Dorry couldn't help feeling joyous. The voices swelled. The room held hundreds of people, and all of them seemed to be singing with all their hearts.

Then a tall, thin man standing at the front lifted his

arm and brought his fingers and thumb together, and that cut off the first strand of the round. One by one, groups dropped out until at last just one girl sang alone, somewhere at the front with a microphone. Her voice was high and sweet and pure, and she lingered on the last line: "—again, I, say, re-joice." Somehow she still sounded joyous, but sad, too, to have to stop singing.

"Thank you, Kate," the man at the front said with a nod. "That was truly a gift of God." His gaze seemed to take in everyone in the room. "Rejoice!" he proclaimed.

"We rejoice indeed!" the crowd agreed enthusiastically. Angela shouted with them.

The man nodded again, accepting the enthusiasm.

"I see seats down front," Angela whispered to Dorry. Dorry followed Angela down the stairs and across a row. People smiled and whispered "Welcome" as they went by. Then the crowd launched into a second song about joy, but faster and more raucous. Someone toward the back started clapping, and soon everyone was. Dorry wasn't much into clapping, but she didn't want to be the only one in the whole place with idle hands, so she joined in. She didn't know the song either, but soon she was singing along with the chorus, "I take joy in the Lord, joy, joy, joy."

There were five or six songs after that, each more rapturous than the last. Beside Dorry, Angela looked absolutely transported. The music buoyed Dorry's spirits, too. She forgot Northview Apartments. She forgot her hair. She forgot Lara and Angela's fight. She forgot the blue sports car. She forgot loneliness. She forgot Bryden. She forgot everything except joy.

Then the man at the front stopped them without leading into a new song. "My time is up," he said. There was an audible groan from the crowd. He smiled. "But it's only seven hours until music vigil tonight. I'd love to see you all there. And Pastor Jim has more wonderful things in store for you now."

The crowd cheered.

He started walking away from the podium, then leaned back. "I almost forgot. For those of you just joining us," he said, "I'm Brother Paul. I'm in charge of the music around here, so if you have any suggestions, any favorite songs the Spirit is calling you to sing tonight or next week, or any time, please let me know."

"He's great," Angela whispered to Dorry. "So talented, but so humble."

As Brother Paul went to his seat, someone else stood up two rows in front of Dorry. "The Lord is good to us!" he shouted without leaving his row.

"We rejoice in the Lord!" the crowd answered

Across the room, another voice rang out. "All our blessings come from God!"

"We rejoice in the Lord!" the crowd repeated.

And then another voice: "Our Father gives us all we need."

And again, the crowd responded, "We rejoice in the Lord."

Dorry remembered something like this from church back in Bryden—what had Reverend Patton called it? Responsive reading? But that had been people mumbling, their tongues tripping over unfamiliar words written in the bulletin. This seemed utterly spontaneous and entirely sincere. There was no script. Everyone around Dorry was shouting and grinning. They seemed truly joyful.

Then Pastor Jim strode to a podium at the front of the room. The crowd was instantly silent, expectant. "'And God saw everything that he had made, and, behold, it was very good,'" he proclaimed. "Genesis 1:31." He paused, giving the biblical words time to resonate. "Brothers and sisters, isn't this a morning made for rejoicing?"

"It is!" some in the crowd cried out.

"We modern Americans, we like to sit around and stew about everything that's wrong with the world. 'Oh, no, there's pollution.' 'Oh, no, the unemployment rate's too high.' 'Oh, no, I've got a history paper due; it's supposed to be twenty-five pages long and I'll actually have to go to the library to do some research.'"

Several people tittered as Pastor Jim made a mock

mournful face. "Oh, yes, you can laugh—but you students out there, you know you say things like that!"

More laughter. Pastor Jim thumped his hand against the podium. "I don't want to imply that there aren't real problems in this world—there are, and we as Fishers have an obligation to be concerned about them. But we also have an obligation to rejoice over all the good things God has given us. We have all the food we need, we have all the clothes we need—some of you girls out there have more clothes than you need, but we won't get into that right now—" Pastor Jim chuckled, and the crowd laughed along with him. "You get the point. And those are just material things. We all know the greatest gift of all is Jesus, who died for our sins. . . ."

Dorry started to tune out Pastor Jim. This was the same old church stuff she'd gotten back in Bryden. She glanced over at Angela, who was listening raptly, her head tilted, in total concentration. Everyone else around her seemed just as fascinated. The crowd that had been so raucous before was absolutely transfixed now.

Then the crowd laughed at something Pastor Jim said, and several people shouted out, "Amen, brother." It reminded Dorry of TV church services—shows she bypassed quickly, flipping through the channels on dull Sunday mornings. She didn't need much imagination to picture Pastor Jim as a TV preacher. Could all these people really have fallen for his act? Dorry looked around again, watching the smiling faces, the radiant expressions. Was something wrong with Dorry that she wasn't transfixed, too?

Pastor Jim finished with a prayer and went to sit down. A trio sang while a bunch of people passed wicker baskets for the collections. Angela leaned over to Dorry and whispered, "Don't worry. New people aren't expected to put anything in. Only believers."

Dorry hadn't planned to put anything in, anyway.

After that, Brother Paul stood again, and led

the crowd in several more songs. Almost against her will, Dorry felt the rising joy again. For as long as the singing lasted, she felt a kinship with everyone in the room. They were all part of one thing, the same song. Dorry joined in again, tentatively at first, then stronger. Angela smiled at her.

This time when Brother Paul brought the singing to a close, he stood still for a few moments, as if in awe. The entire room was silent. No one coughed or whispered or, it seemed, moved at all. Dorry could hear the hum of the room's ventilation unit. "I felt the Spirit in your singing," Brother Paul said softly. Then with a flourish, he shouted, "Rejoice!" He thrust his right arm high in the air, as if raising a sword.

That one word seemed to break the spell in the room.

People stood up, began to chatter. Someone tapped Dorry on the shoulder. "Hello. Are you a friend of Angela's? I'm Susan."

"I'm Joyce," someone else said. "Glad you could come."

Dorry lost track of names after that, but at least a dozen people greeted her and introduced themselves.

"Are you going to Fellowship Hour?" one of the girls said. Dorry thought her name was Elizabeth.

"Want to?" Angela asked. "It's coffee, juice, and doughnuts. Stuff like that." Dorry looked at her watch. Her parents were expecting her home for Sunday dinner, and it was already eleven. If Fellowship Hour really lasted an hour, she'd be late. "We don't have to stay long," Angela said.

"Okay," Dorry agreed. She followed the others out of the auditorium into another room with a fancy glass chandelier. There were two tables with coffee, tea, several juices, doughnut holes, and cut-up fruit. Several chairs were scattered about the room, but most people were standing. Everyone seemed to be with lifelong friends, chattering away happily. Dorry felt a pang. How long would it take her to be that comfortable with her friends? But Angela and Joyce and Susan and the others surrounded her, laughing and talking all at once. They all seemed to know each other already, but they wanted to know everything about Dorry.

"Angela said you just moved here from Ohio?" Susan asked.

"Yes," Dorry said. Then it was easy to talk, to tell her story and let the others sympathize. They all got doughnuts and juice. It was a happy moment.

Suddenly Pastor Jim was beside her. "Dorry!" he said, touching her arm lightly. "I'm so glad you could come. What did you think of the service?"

Dorry tried to find a good answer. How could she tell a minister she wasn't really into religion? Then, as if prompting an awkward preschooler, Angela said, "You seemed to like the music a lot."

"Yes," Dorry said. "I did."

Pastor Jim nodded appreciatively. "It was awe-inspiring this morning, wasn't it? Sometimes I think that's the closest we'll ever get to heaven on earth, listening to wonderful music. Do you sing or play any musical instruments?"

"No," Dorry said. "My sister's the musical one. My dad refused to pay for lessons for me because he said I'd just quit when I discovered boys. That's what my sister did." Now, why had she said that? It made her dad sound like an ogre. Which he wasn't, of course.

Pastor Jim was nodding sympathetically. "It's tough being a parent," he said. "And it's tough following siblings who sometimes seem to mess up your chances for, shall we say, the riches of life."

"Oh, it wasn't that bad," Dorry hastened to add. "By the time I came along, my parents were just plain tired. They thought they were done raising children. I was a mistake." Dorry said it flippantly. She wanted to be as joking and casual as everybody else at the Fellowship Hour. But Pastor Jim gave her a look aching with compassion.

"Oh, you should *never* say that, even in jest," he said. "Even if your earthly parents didn't intend your existence, God did. He must have a special purpose in mind for you. Remember Sarah and Abraham? The child God gave them in their old age was the blessing of their lives, and the beginning of the entire Hebrew people."

Dorry had to look away from his strange, piercing eyes. She couldn't remember exactly who Sarah and Abraham were, but hearing Pastor Jim tell her that God had a special purpose for her made her feel funny. Her heart beat fast and her face felt hot. She wanted to say, "Oh, no, it never bothered me that I was a mistake," but suddenly it seemed that it always had. And maybe Pastor Jim had now cured that hurt she'd carried around all her life, without even realizing it. Why had her parents said that to her—"You were a mistake"? Didn't they know how it would hurt? Why hadn't they told her she had a special purpose? Pastor Jim lay his hand gently on Dorry's shoulder.

"Bless you," he said tenderly. "You'll be back."

CHAPTER SEVEN

TWO WEEKS LATER, DORRY sat in a van with Brad and Angela and a bunch of other kids riding to the Fishers Annual Fall Retreat.

"Come on—you'll have fun," Angela had said, inviting her in the hall between classes one day.

It was a constant refrain, the line that had lured Dorry to two weeks' worth of Fishers parties and pizza dinners and even a repeat of the Sunday service. Regardless of what she thought about religion, Dorry was usually easily persuaded. Anything beat sitting in the apartment alone while her parents worked. Even the retreat seemed perfectly timed—it fell on a weekend when both her parents were working Saturday. Still, Dorry hesitantly protested, "But I'm not really a Fisher. . . ."

Angela playfully slugged her. "Oh, that doesn't matter. We like you. Remember?"

She could hardly forget, they reminded her so often. Dorry liked her new friends—of course she did—but she still thought they were a little strange. She'd noticed the other kids at Crestwood made fun of them sometimes, snickering when the Fishers bowed their heads and prayed over lunch. Now that Dorry knew about Fishers, they didn't hesitate to pray in front of her. Sitting between Angela and Brad, her own head resolutely unbowed, Dorry was always torn between wanting to assure the rest of the Crestwood students, "Look, just because I'm sitting with them, it doesn't mean I'm as crazy as they are," and wanting to defend the Fishers, "Hey, they may be different, but at least they're nice. They talked to me when none of you would." Of course, she knew no one else at Crestwood cared about her, one way or another. And the Fishers did. Why else would Angela look so delighted when Dorry agreed to come to the retreat?

Now Angela was leaning toward the window. "Just wait till you see the Lakeland Hills lodge. Oh! There it is—"

Dorry turned and stared. The building in front of them was stunning. Nestled among a grove of trees vibrant with autumn colors, the lodge had balconies on every level and gingerbread trim on the roof. It looked very expensive. She wondered how Fishers could put on the retreat "totally free," as Angela had assured her.

"Come on." Angela tugged on Dorry's arm. "Inside's even nicer." Everyone else was climbing out of the van, mingling with kids from the other three vans that had driven behind them. Except for Brad and Angela, she didn't know anyone else. She thought she'd seen a couple of the kids at Fishers services, but she wasn't sure.

"I'll get your suitcase," Brad said.

"What about your own?" Dorry asked, even as she felt a thrill of pleasure that he seemed more concerned about her than himself.

"My own? I travel light, my dear," Brad said in his joking tone. "I have the clothes on my back—what more do I need?"

"Everything you dropped off last night," Angela said, laughing.

As they all jumped out of the van, the door of the lodge swung open and Pastor Jim stepped out. "Welcome, all," he proclaimed. "Let the fall retreat begin!"

It was so formal Dorry had to laugh, and so did several others. She smiled at a shy-looking boy with glasses and he smiled back. She felt her already-high spirits zoom skyward. She took a deep breath of the crisp fall air and felt like she was inhaling pure joy.

"Come in, come in," Pastor Jim urged.

They all traipsed in. The main floor of the lodge was

open, with sliding-glass doors at the back leading to a deck. Dorry gasped at the view beyond: a deep, heavily wooded ravine. It was incredible. She hadn't known that flat, flat Indiana had such scenery.

Pastor Jim let the full impact of the sight sink in before speaking. "Do you know each other well after the drive?"

People muttered no's.

He shook his head sorrowfully. "And you're all such wonderful people. . . . Janelle here is a talented musician who has the voice of an angel. I've heard that Sam is a better joke teller than any so-called comedians on TV. Dorry just moved here from a small town in Ohio, Bryden, and she's already gladdening the hearts of her many new friends at Crestwood High . . ."

He went on naming names and giving brief descriptions, touching each person lightly on the arm as he went around the room. He seemed to know everyone well. Dorry concentrated on matching names and faces. The boy with glasses who'd smiled at her outside was introduced as Zachary, and he was billed as a scientific genius.

"Anyone remember everyone's name?" Pastor Jim asked at the end.

Dorry thought she did. But before she could decide if she was going to speak up, Pastor Jim went on.

"Anyone remember just one other person's name?"

"Sure," several people said.

"Janelle, then," Pastor Jim said. "Say your name and one other."

"I'm Janelle," she said, and pointed, "and that's Bob."

Then Bob named himself and Janelle and Lisa. Then it was Lisa's turn. The group went on, adding one name to the list every time. Dorry came in at about the eleventh name, and managed to name everyone without embarrassing herself. The group broke into applause for the last person, a girl named Sarah, who rattled off the names without pausing for breath.

"You forgot someone," Pastor Jim said, clowning a pout and pointing to himself.

"Oops—and that's Pastor Jim," Sarah said.

"So it's my turn now," Pastor Jim said. He went around saying everyone's name again slowly. His resonant voice caressed each word. Dorry felt bad for having thought he was like a TV evangelist, someone who stood in a studio somewhere and pretended he was talking to real people, not blank air. Pastor Jim obviously cared deeply about each one of them. If Dorry ever had a boyfriend, she'd want him to say her name the way Pastor Jim did. "And there's still one name we've left out," Pastor Jim said. "Does anybody know it?"

Everyone looked around, puzzled.

"An important name," Pastor Jim added.

"God," Zachary said. "Or Jesus."

"Close," Pastor Jim said. "The Holy Spirit. The part of the Trinity that is with us always. When He appeared to His disciples after His death, Jesus promised they would never be alone, and it is the Holy Spirit that true believers can rely on always."

Pastor Jim went on about the Holy Spirit at some length, but it didn't seem like a sermon or a lecture. It was more like he was sharing news that mattered a great deal to him, and he was eager for everyone else to know it, too. For once, Dorry didn't mind hearing about religion. She wondered what it was like to be Pastor Jim, so sure that he was never alone.

The rest of the day passed in a blur. There were other games and skits and a hike in the woods and pizza for dinner. Then there were more games and a late-night snack of popcorn and hot chocolate. Nobody seemed to want to go to bed. By one a.m. they were all sitting around the lodge fireplace talking about God.

"Do you ever wonder how God could really be in charge of everything?" a girl named Danielle asked. "What's it called? Omni-something."

"Omnipotent," Brad supplied the word, and pretended to take a mini bow for his own brilliance.

"See, that's where I have my problems with God," said another girl, Moira. "I think I'd like Him better if He weren't in charge."

"Why?" Angela asked.

"Because there are so many bad things in the world. Think about people dying of AIDS, or cancer, or starving to death in Africa. If God's really in charge, and He's supposed to be a good guy, how come there's so much suffering?"

Everyone was silent. Dorry waited for Pastor Jim to answer from the back of the crowd where he was lounging. She was curious what he'd say. But the next voice wasn't Pastor Jim's resonant one.

"It's because of free choice," Zachary said. His voice was thin and reedy, but echoed in the huge lodge. "You know, after Eve ate from the tree of the knowledge of good and evil, God gave humans the power to make choices in their lives. It naturally follows that if some of our choices are bad, bad things happen." He shrugged, as if it were just an academic point.

"So if bad things happen to you, it's your fault?" Moira said. She was sitting up straight now. "My little brother got leukemia, and was on chemotherapy for a long time and then . . . then he died anyway. What did a six-year-old do that he deserved to die?" She ended with a whimper that was almost crying.

Because he was right behind her, Dorry heard Zachary's answer: "No, I don't mean it was your brother's fault. Maybe it was the fault of everybody else, society as a whole, that we haven't worked hard enough to find a cure for cancer. Why do we spend so much on, I don't know, sports, when the same money could save a lot of lives?"

Dorry had never thought of things that way. She wondered if Zachary was right. But she didn't think many others heard him because Angela was speaking, her voice ringing clearly through the lodge.

"We all deserve to die," she said. "The Bible says, 'All have sinned and fall short of the glory of God.' Even six-year-olds. Even newborn babies, because of original sin. It's the grace of God that saves us from eternal death, eternal separation from God."

Now Moira really was crying. "So God *did* kill my brother."

"No," Angela said, more gently. "Death happens because of evil. God offers us a way out of evil, a chance to live with Him forever without sin. All we must do is accept Jesus' gift of salvation."

The lodge was quiet again, except for Moira's sobs. Dorry looked around. The others all sat frozen, looking uncomfortable. Dorry thought everyone must be feeling the same as she was: embarrassed at witnessing Moira's grief, not sure what to do. She wished there were something she could say to help.

And then, suddenly, Moira's sobs ceased. "I feel—I see it—Oh my God!" She breathed in sharply.

"What? What?" several kids said at once.

Moira didn't answer. Her face had gone very pale. Her dark eyes were unfocused, as if she were gazing far beyond the crowd and the lodge. She inhaled again, but slowly and steadily this time, ending with a beatific smile. Her eyes slid closed and she dropped her head as if in a trance. Then, slowly, she opened her eyes again. "Yes," she breathed, still smiling peacefully. Her eyes were focused now, but she seemed oblivious to everyone's stares.

"What happened?" Angela said.

"I think I saw . . . I saw God," Moira said calmly. "He spoke to me. He said . . . I can't really explain. It wasn't like words."

"But what did it feel like?" Angela persisted.

"Love," Moira said. "He told me He loves me."

Dorry couldn't believe her eyes. How could someone go from crying that hard to being totally calm so suddenly? For Moira seemed absolutely at peace. A nuclear bomb could land at her feet, Dorry thought, and she'd go to her death still smiling that tranquil smile.

But just as abruptly as she'd changed before, Moira suddenly gasped, her smile gone. She held her hand over her face. "Oh, no," she moaned. "Oh, no. He can't love me. . . ."

"What are you talking about?" Angela asked.

"In the hospital—when my brother was dying—"

Moira spoke in spurts, barely coherent. "I ran out of his room—I yelled at God—'I hate you! I hate you!' It was sin, the worst sin of all—"

"Moira, Moira." Pastor Jim spoke from the back of the room, his voice resounding with empathy. "Don't you know that when you accept Jesus, all your sins are washed clean? Then you are clean enough to live with God forever, to be worthy of His love. Is that what you want, to accept Jesus' sacrifice and be saved for all eternity?"

"Oh, yes," Moira breathed. "I want to be saved."

And then her smile was back. Angela walked over and gave her a deep embrace. Pastor Jim followed, and then others were lining up, hugging her and murmuring congratulations.

Dorry hung back, not sure if she should hug Moira or not. Nothing like this had ever happened at Bryden Methodist. She looked around, and several other kids looked uncertain, too. That made her feel a bond with them. Dorry could never have told anyone else exactly what she'd witnessed. She could picture Marissa saying, "This girl did *what*?" But everyone around her had seen it, too.

The hugging ended, and everyone began singing. Moira sat there the rest of the night looking absolutely joyful. Dorry kept sneaking wondering glances at her. *Had* she seen God? What had it been like?

CHAPTER EIGHT

IT WAS THREE THIRTY A.M. before everyone began heading for bed.

Brushing her teeth in the communal bathroom, Dorry whispered with some of the other girls about Moira's conversion.

"I've never seen anything like it," Dorry said.

"It was like a movie," one of the others, Janelle, said, spitting out a mouthful of toothpaste. "Except she wasn't acting."

"Have any of you ever felt that close to God?" Angela asked.

Everyone shook their heads.

"I have," Angela said.

And if Dorry had envied Angela before because she was rich and pretty and good friends with Brad, she wondered now if maybe there wasn't more to it. If she wanted Angela's confidence and self-possession, maybe she also had to have Angela's God.

"How—" someone started to ask.

Angela brushed her hair in long, flowing strokes. "Just turn your life over to God. He'll reward you abundantly."

"That's too simple," someone protested. "Sure, it's easy to say, but—"

"And it's easy to do," Angela said firmly. "You must turn over everything to God, wholeheartedly." She flipped her hair over her shoulder and began gathering up her toothbrush, toothpaste, washcloth, and towel. She walked toward the door then, hand on the knob, turned around. "Pray about it tonight. We'll talk more in the morning."

After Angela left, Dorry waited for someone to start making fun of her. She had sounded so sincere. If this had been a group of kids back in Bryden, people wouldn't have even waited for her to go before they began laughing. But nobody was laughing now.

"See you tomorrow," Janelle said, following Angela out the door.

"You too," the others muttered, subdued.

Dorry wasn't sure if she was just tired or still awed, but she seemed to notice everything with heightened senses: the row of faces reflected in the mirror, the smell of skin cream, the hum of the lights overhead. Even her toothpaste tasted different. Had witnessing Moira's transformation somehow changed Dorry, too? Did she want it to? She finished brushing her teeth and left, too. She was sharing a room with Angela, and she didn't want to bother Angela if she was already in bed.

But Angela was kneeling beside her bed, hands folded, head bowed, eyes closed, lips moving. With her hair cascading over her shoulders, she looked like an old-fashioned portrait of a little girl saying bedtime prayers. Dorry wasn't sure what to do. Was it rude to walk in on someone's prayers? Should she wait in the hall until Angela was done? Or should she just climb into bed and pretend she hadn't noticed? But surely it would be rude not to say good night.

Dorry cleared her throat. Angela didn't look up. Dorry watched, curious now about prayer. Angela's face was solemn as she spoke silently. Then her mouth was still and she seemed to be listening to an answer. She kept her head bowed and eyes closed. Then she smiled and began praying again. Dorry wished she knew how to read lips. After a few minutes, she tiptoed to her bed and climbed in. She was asleep before Angela finished her prayer.

In the morning Dorry was awakened by someone with a wonderful voice singing, "Morning Has Broken" in the hallway. Her watch said it was only seven thirty, and all she wanted to do was go back to sleep. But when she looked over at Angela's bed she saw that Angela was already up and gone. Something like guilt drove her to stumble out of bed and to the bathroom. Angela was there, rubbing a towel on her wet hair.

"Sleep well?" she asked.

"Mmm," Dorry answered groggily. "Do we *have* to get up now?"

"Of course not," Angela said. "But you don't want to miss breakfast or any of the fun, do you?"

She looked so concerned—so potentially disappointed—that Dorry mumbled "No" and went to get her shower things.

Saturday passed much as Friday afternoon and evening had, with games and laughter and food, and discussions of God cropping up at every turn. Dorry had tuned out most of the religious talk at other Fishers events, but now she was fascinated by every mention. The whole group played kickball on a huge field by the lodge, and Brad accused the boy serving as ref of "legalism" when he called him out.

"Do you think we're saved by works instead of grace?" Brad said. "Are you trying to earn your salvation by being the perfect ref?"

"No. But don't you believe in confessing your sins? Just admit you're out, and I won't have to judge you," the other boy said.

"Okay," Brad said. "You're absolutely right. I will be meek about it." He raised his face to the sky and shouted, "Hear that, God? Doesn't that mean I get to inherit the earth?"

Dorry wasn't sure exactly what they meant, but for the first time in her life, she began to see how religion might relate to everything. It wasn't just something that belonged in church, something you mumbled about for an hour on Sunday morning (maybe), and then forgot about the rest of the week. She was so busy thinking about that notion that she missed the ball when it came zooming right toward her in left field. She braced herself for the inevitable, "Idiot!"—or worse—someone was sure to yell at her, the way people had in every other game of kickball she'd ever played. But nobody screamed. Instead, Moira, who was pitching, shrugged and smiled sympathetically, and Angela ran over and patted her on the back.

"Better luck next time," she said encouragingly.

Dorry thought what a wonderful place the world would be if everyone were a Fisher, if everyone lived by the words in the Bible.

By nightfall, Dorry had practically forgotten there was a world outside the retreat. She felt as though she'd known the other kids forever. They had their own inside jokes, even their own pet names. People had begun calling Dorry "Chocolate," or just "Choc," because when

Pastor Jim had asked them to imagine heaven and hell at lunchtime, she'd said, "I guess there'd be a lot of chocolate in heaven, and none in hell." It'd gotten a good laugh, a friendly laugh.

After dinner, everyone gathered by the fireplace again. But tonight, Pastor Jim strode to the front right away and leaned against the wood mantel. "You like each other, don't you?" he began.

The group laughed. Brad pointed at Angela and joked, "Everyone but her!" She threw a pillow at him.

Pastor Jim let the hilarity die down. "The reason I ask is because if you are to become Fishers, to devote your life to God, you must also devote yourself to your brothers and sisters in Christ. They are to be everything to you: your counselors, your confidantes, your forgiveness, your friends. You must trust them absolutely, with your life."

Dorry wanted to stop him and protest, "Wait a minute. I never said I wanted to become a Fisher." But maybe she did. Did she? She didn't speak. Everyone else sat silent, too, waiting.

"There's a game we play—it's more than a game, really, almost a test." Pastor Jim pointed into the crowd, moving his hand slowly in a circle. Dorry felt a thrill of fear when he pointed to her, but he kept going. At last he stopped, pointing directly at Moira. "Moira," he said in a low, confidential tone. Dorry had to lean in to hear. "We witnessed the birth of your faith in God last night. Do you also have faith in your fellow Fishers?"

"I do," she replied. Dorry had been to weddings where the bride and groom responded less solemnly.

"Are you willing to do anything to prove it?"

"I am."

He held his hand out to her. She clasped it and rose gracefully. "Come," he said.

Others began standing up, so Dorry did, too. Pastor Jim led Moira to the huge, open staircase in the middle of the lodge. He signaled for everyone else to stay at the bottom. He and Moira climbed to the top. Pastor Jim whispered something to her, then turned to the crowd.

"Jason?" he called.

A burly boy weaved through the crowd and mounted the stairs. He joined Pastor Jim on the fourth step down. Moira stood at the very top, facing away from Pastor Jim and Jason. Only her toes touched the floor. The heels of her boots hung in empty air above the step below.

"I ask you again—do you trust us?" Pastor Jim's voice rang out, echoing against the lodge's cathedral ceiling.

"Yes."

"Will you prove it?"

"Yes."

And then, without so much as a glance over her shoulder, Moira let herself fall backward. Dorry wasn't the only one who gasped, picturing Moira's thin body tumbling down the dozens of stairs. But before her head hit the first step, Pastor Jim and Jason had her in their arms. There was a cry of relief from the crowd. Pastor Jim and Jason took turns hugging Moira. Then they released her and she turned toward the crowd. Dorry saw that there were tears streaming down her face, but with her victorious smile, they looked like tears of joy.

"Janelle?" Pastor Jim called.

There were whispers in the crowd, as everyone realized that others were going to be asked to fall. Dorry stepped aside as Janelle, looking white-faced but resolute, pushed toward the stairs. Two others, a boy named Mark and a girl named Becky, joined her at the bottom. They climbed the stairs together. Janelle's "I am" and "I do" sounded more frightened than Moira's, but she let herself fall without hesitation. Mark and Becky caught her and hugged her just as carefully and joyously as Pastor Jim and Jason had hugged Moira.

"Not me. Please, God, not me," Dorry prayed without quite realizing what she was doing.

Seven others went, falling and being caught in turn. Then Pastor Jim called Dorry's name. Blood pounded in her ears. Brad and Angela stepped up behind her. Angela put her hand on Dorry's back, gently guiding her forward. Dorry wanted to protest, to say no. But how could she?

She'd look like a coward. Brad and Angela would think she didn't trust them. She stumbled toward the stairs. Her legs trembled as she climbed. Brad and Angela were on either side of her, each holding an arm to steady her. Then they let go, and Dorry realized she was at the top. Brad and Angela backed away. She couldn't see them behind her.

I hate heights, she wanted to say. I don't have to do this, do I? Maybe she could make it into a joke, say something like, "I'd rather have chocolate." But everyone else had been totally serious. The somber mood in the room felt like a weight on her chest.

Angela's clear voice asked behind her, "Do you trust us?"

"Yes," Dorry mumbled.

"Are you willing to stake your life to prove it?"

"Yes," Dorry mumbled again.

And then Dorry was supposed to fall backward, but she couldn't make herself do it. She remembered once when she'd been nine or ten, and Marissa had talked her into going up on the high dive at the Bryden pool. She'd stood at the edge of the diving board, looking down at the blue, blue water, which seemed miles away. All she was supposed to do then was jump, feet first, facing forward, but she hadn't been able to. She'd backed down the ladder in shame, jeers ringing in her ears from the older boys waiting in line behind her.

"Dorry," Angela said behind her, so softly that probably no one below them heard. "We want you to be one of us. But if you aren't willing to trust us, we can't trust you."

Dorry squeezed her eyes shut and tilted her head back. Before she had decided if she was going to let herself fall entirely, Brad and Angela's hands were on her back, lifting her up. She was safe. It was over. Dorry wanted to cry and laugh all at once. Angela hugged her tight, and then Brad did, too, just as if she'd really fallen, really proven her trust. They held her hands climbing down the stairs. Their hands were warm and strong. She felt like a little girl safe between her parents. She felt overwhelmed with relief and joy and—though she tried to hide it—shame. Why hadn't she let herself fall? She did trust Brad and Angela, didn't she?

Dorry barely watched the others repeat the ritual. Everything seemed to be happening at a great distance. Even if someone had fallen without being caught, had tumbled down the stairs and landed right at her feet, she wouldn't have had the energy to help them, or even to step back and let someone else help.

At the end, Pastor Jim went around hugging everyone who had been caught. Then he stood back and proclaimed, "You are all ready."

His words were like a blessing.

He led them all out the back door of the lodge, down

the steps from the deck, and into the dark ravine. Dorry stumbled over roots and rocks, but every time she almost fell, Brad or Angela caught her arm. Finally, when the crowd stood at the bottom of the ravine, beside a roaring brook, Pastor Jim stopped them.

"The early Christians met in the catacombs of Rome," he said. "It was probably about this dark."

High overhead, practically hidden by trees, Dorry could see a thin moon. It went behind a cloud.

"But Christians, true Christians, are not afraid of the dark. We know the true light." Pastor Jim struck a match and it sprang to life. He touched the match to a candle and the glow lit up his face.

"All of you know about the salvation Jesus offers you. You know that you are steeped in sin, that, as you are, you are filthy and despicable and unfit for the sight of God. You know that only Jesus' intercession, his mercy and sacrifice, can redeem you. He said, 'I am the way and the truth and the life; no one comes to the Father, but by me.' He said, 'You must be born anew.' Will you come? Will you renounce your former life, your sin, and your evil and be born anew?"

Dorry thought about getting rid of her shame over not truly falling into Brad and Angela's arms. And beyond that—if she was born again, would she be free of feeling fat and ugly and undesirable? Would she be as happy as all the Fishers? Maybe they weren't crazy, as she'd thought. They just focused on what was truly important—God.

Nobody spoke. Pastor Jim placed the candle on a rock. "This will be our altar," he said. "Will you come forward and leave your sin behind? Do you accept Jesus as your Lord and Savior? Will you be cleansed for all eternity?"

"I will," a girl called out. She stepped forward and Dorry saw that it was Janelle.

Others followed, tentatively at first, then in bunches. They crowded around the rock, kneeling and praying.

Dorry bowed her head. "God?" she called silently. "Will you save me?" She didn't hear a clear voice, the way Angela evidently did. But she suddenly felt a sense of peacefulness like she'd never felt before. She wasn't worried about anything anymore. Was this what the Holy Spirit was like?

Angela gently pushed her forward. "You're ready, Dorry."

Dorry knelt with the others. Pastor Jim lay his hand on Dorry's head and called out, "Dorry Stevens, your sins are forgiven. You are a new creation. 'The old has passed away, behold, the new has come.'"

And it really seemed that it had, that she was a new person.

Dorry wasn't sure how long she knelt there, not really praying, not even thinking. She was barely aware of Pastor Jim laying his hand on others' heads, calling out the same words. Then on some cue Dorry missed, everyone began standing up. Someone started singing, "We Are Climbing Jacob's Ladder," then "Kum Ba Yah" and other songs. Pastor Jim led them out of the ravine a different, flatter way. When they reached a road, the Fishers' vans were there waiting. Pastor Jim directed them to climb in.

"Where are we going?" Dorry whispered to Angela.

"Ssh," Angela said. "Don't talk. Trust us."

In the van there was more singing. Dorry tried to hold on to the feeling she'd had when Pastor Jim laid his hand on her head, that she was totally forgiven, totally pure, and totally clean. She must not do anything bad or think anything bad again.

The van stopped and Dorry realized with a jolt that they were at the apartment-complex clubhouse where the Fishers' parties had been. She turned to Angela and started to ask, "Wh—" Angela silenced her with a shake of her head.

Everyone trouped into the clubhouse. What seemed like hundreds of people were silently waiting for them. Dorry passed through a gauntlet of hugs, mostly from people she barely recognized or didn't know. But the feeling of love and belonging was overwhelming. She was surprised to end up by the side of the indoor pool. Pastor

Jim was in the shallow end, the water halfway up the legs of his jeans.

"The Bible says, 'Repent and be baptized,'" he proclaimed, his voice echoing in the atrium over the pool. "Jesus himself was baptized by his cousin, JoŸ the Baptist, in the River Jordan. If you are to follow Christ, you must do the same."

Becky and Mark led Janelle down the steps into the water.

Dorry watched, puzzled. "Angela," she whispered. "I—"

"Shh," Angela hissed. Others around them turned to stare.

"No, I have to tell you this," Dorry insisted. "I've already been baptized. When I was a baby. So I shouldn't do it again, should I? It'd be a sin or something, wouldn't it?"

"No." Angela shook her head, and whispered back. "Infant baptism is wrong. If you aren't baptized in Fishers, you're going to hell."

Dorry considered that. She didn't remember being baptized, and she'd certainly never felt like this before. Angela knew a lot more about religion than Dorry did.

"Dorry," Pastor Jim called. Dorry stepped forward. Angela and Brad walked into the water on either side of her. The smell of chlorine filled her nose and she held back a sneeze, but the water was warm and inviting. She wondered if the River Jordan had been cold or hot—it certainly hadn't smelled of chlorine. Then she pushed away those thoughts because she was supposed to be thinking about God.

"Dorry Stevens, do you renounce all sin and evil?" Pastor Jim asked.

"Yes," she said.

"Do you accept Jesus Christ as your Lord and Savior?"

"Yes."

"Do you accept the love and dominion of the Fishers of Men, as the representative of God's mission on earth?"

Dorry blinked, trying to comprehend his words. Everyone was waiting. "Yes," she said.

"And do you vow to dedicate your life to God as embodied in Fishers? Do you vow to forsake all outsiders and all worldly pursuits and endeavors for the good of God's kingdom?"

"Yes," Dorry said again, not stopping to think this time. That was what everyone expected.

Then Pastor Jim was pushing her down, down, into the warm water. She forgot to take a breath and came up sputtering. Water dripped from her hair. Brad and Angela led her out of the pool and wrapped her in warm towels, handling her as tenderly as a baby. Dorry noticed that, though they were both wet up to the waist, they did nothing for themselves. The three of them stood on the edge of the pool, arms around each other, watching the rest of the baptisms.

"Welcome to Fishers," Angela said gently. Her lips brushed Dorry's cheek, almost like a kiss.

CHAPTER NINE

AFTER THE BAPTISMS, DORRY felt like a new baby chick, freshly hatched from its egg. But no chicken had ever felt such joy—or been greeted so happily. She couldn't stop grinning as people told her, over and over again, "Welcome, welcome. You are God's child." It was after two a.m. before the retreat group got into the vans and went back to the lodge, but people still lingered downstairs by the fireplace for another hour or two, reliving the evening.

"If I die tonight, I will die happy," someone said.

"If I live a million years, I will never forget this night," someone else said.

Dorry kept quiet, afraid that speaking would destroy her fragile euphoria. She couldn't possibly explain how she felt.

When they finally went up to bed, Angela said, "Here, I'll show you how to pray."

So Dorry knelt beside Angela, Angela showing her the proper angle to tilt her head, the proper way to fold her hands. Angela began praying out loud: "Dear God, we rejoice in the salvation of my new sister, Dorry. Thank you for your wisdom in choosing her and making her one of your own. Please make her a worthy member of your flock. Allow her to grow in wisdom and faith. . . ."

Dorry nodded off before Angela was finished, but Angela didn't get upset. She gently shook Dorry and helped her to bed.

The next morning, Angela woke Dorry to pray beside her again. "You must do this every morning and every evening, to stay connected to God," Angela said. It was very early, and Dorry was still very tired. She couldn't listen to all of Angela's long prayer. Suddenly she realized Angela had stopped talking.

"Your turn," Angela said, without looking up.

"I—I—" Dorry stuttered. "I, uh, thank you, God, for this . . . day. Thanks for saving me. Um, please bless everybody. Amen."

Dorry knew it was a pathetic prayer. She opened one eye and peeked at Angela, but Angela only resumed her own prayer, her words flowing evenly as a brook. When she'd said her own "amen" and gracefully stood up, she patted Dorry on the back.

"It takes a while to learn how to pray right," she said. "I'll give you a list of what to say."

The rest of the retreat passed as hazily as a dream. At breakfast some of the others talked about going to the Fishers' big Sunday service downtown, but in the end they all agreed it would be better to worship alone as one small group. They wanted nothing to disturb them. The honking of one horn in city traffic might jolt them out of savoring their salvation. At the lodge, everyone spoke in soft voices, moved slowly, touched gently. They all understood.

At six o'clock, when it was time to leave, Dorry gave in to tears, hugging everyone good-bye. "I'll miss you," she cried to Janelle.

"Good grief, you'll all see each other at Fishers functions. Maybe as soon as tomorrow," Brad said. "No one's moving to Siberia." But Dorry thought she saw a tear glinting in his eye, too.

The vans took them back to their schools. Angela had promised to take Dorry home from there. The huge, modern Crestwood High School looked different than it had on Friday—not nearly as scary and overwhelming. Of course, Dorry knew it was she who was different. She was a Fisher now. She had God on her side. She had nothing to fear.

"I'm over here," Angela said, leading Dorry to the student parking lot behind the building.

Dorry squinted into the distance. She didn't see the Mercedes. The lot was deserted except for a bright blue sports car that reminded Dorry of the car she'd seen at Northview so long ago—had it been just a month? It seemed a lifetime ago. And in one sense it was. Dorry had a whole new life now. How could she have ever suspected Angela of hiding from her? She'd been so insecure, so distrustful.

"Where—" she started to ask.

Angela was striding toward the sports car, unlocking its doors. "I don't have the Mercedes. That's my dad's. This is my car—it was in the shop for a while."

Dorry froze, confused, a few steps away. Her thoughts raced. So it had been Angela that day at Northview. So she had lied to Dorry about being there. Or not really lied—Dorry had never actually asked her. But surely she'd given Angela every chance to tell her she was there, to explain why she'd hidden from Dorry. Why *had* she hidden? And what should Dorry do now? Say something about the car? Pretend nothing had happened?

"You saw me that day at your apartment complex, didn't you?" Angela asked quietly.

Dorry didn't know what to say. She settled on the truth.

"Yes."

"I thought so."

Somehow, Angela didn't seem upset, or worried that Dorry would be upset. She let Dorry into the car, but didn't put the keys into the ignition yet. They sat still. Dorry waited. Finally Angela turned to her and began talking, her eyes locked on Dorry's. "You see, when there's someone who shows a great deal of promise as a potential Fisher, we like to check them out, so we don't say anything to scare them away. Let me give you an example. My parents are divorced, and divorce is evil and wrong. I know that now, because I know the truth. But before I saw the light, if I had heard anyone from Fishers condemning divorced people, it would have upset me. And the Devil would have used my anger, so that in my blindness, I probably would have missed my chance for eternal life."

"But—"

Angela patted Dorry's hand. "That first day we met you, we could tell you were crying out for salvation. And, too, we could see that you could become a wonderful Fisher, possibly a leader in the group. So I followed your bus to see where you'd get off, to know more about you."

Dorry was trying to make sense of it all. As a Fisher, what was she supposed to say? She didn't know, so she said what she wanted. "But why did you hide from me?"

"I didn't want you to think I was *spying* on you," Angela said, as though that should have been obvious. "I didn't think you would understand then. And after that,

I made sure you didn't see this car because I didn't want the Devil to use any doubts you might have. But now, now that you've been saved, you can see things with the eyes of God. I know that you have enough faith now."

Dorry struggled to be as filled with faith as Angela thought she was. Questions whispered in the back of her mind—Why did it matter where she lived? If following her home wasn't spying, what was it? But Dorry resolutely shut out every doubt. How could she think badly of Angela? They were sisters now, fellow Fishers. Angela was the one who'd led her to salvation. Dorry owed her very soul to Angela.

Angela was smiling. "God was testing you, letting you see the car. But I can tell you've passed the test. You are a good and faithful child of God." She leaned over and impulsively gave Dorry a hug. "I'll take you home now. I'm sure you're tired."

Angela did most of the talking all the way to Northview. She chattered about what Dorry would do, now that she was a Fisher. "You'll be in a Bible Study, of course. And then there's the discipling sessions three times a week—did I tell you I get to be your discipler? And—"

"What's a discipler?" Dorry asked, roused from watching road signs flash by.

"It's like, well, a big sister in the faith. Someone who shows you how to grow as a Fisher."

"Oh," Dorry said. If she hadn't been so tired, she would have asked more. But they were pulling into Northview now. Angela parked right beside Dorry's father's car.

"My parents are home for once," Dorry said.

"That's good," Angela said. "You must tell them the minute you walk in the door about becoming a Fisher. Pray with them, and maybe the Lord will see fit to save them, too."

Dorry shifted uncomfortably in the bucket seat. Somehow she hadn't thought that far ahead. It was one thing to be a Fisher among other Fishers, but she didn't know how her parents would react. Maybe they would notice a difference in her before she told them anything. She would be really good and kind and they would understand what a glorious thing had happened.

Dorry opened the door. Her father was sitting at the kitchen table eating a sandwich. He looked old and sunken and defeated. Maybe Angela was right, and she should tell him about Fishers right away—he needed to be saved, too. But he would be the harder parent to tell.

"Where's Mom?" she asked. "She didn't get called in to work, did she?"

He looked up, startled, as if he hadn't heard her come in. "No," he said in a strange, flat voice. "She's in the hospital. She had a heart attack."

CHAPTER TEN

"WHAT?" DORRY SAID. "IS she—" She was too scared to finish the thought.

"She's all right," her father said quietly. "Won't be in the hospital but a few more days. Docs said it was pretty mild, we should just see it like a warning light for a car engine." But his face didn't look like he thought everything was all right.

Dorry dropped her suitcase and sat down because her knees were trembling. "When—"

"Friday afternoon, when she was getting ready for work," her father said. "She had these shooting pains in her chest."

"You should have let me know." Dorry wondered what she'd been doing when it happened. Laughing and talking in the van with Brad and Angela? Playing games to learn the other kids' names? She should have been with her mother.

"Weren't nothing you could do," Dorry's dad said. "Your mom said it was best to leave you where you could have some fun."

Dorry shook her head, not to disagree, but to clear her mind. She didn't know what to think. How could this have happened just when she was so happy about becoming a Fisher?

"Can I go see her?" she asked.

Dorry's dad looked at his watch. "Visiting hours are over. I'll take you tomorrow. You can call." He gave her the number and went to the couch to watch TV. Dorry dialed the number with shaking fingers.

"Mom?"

"Hey, sweetie."

The voice was weak but blessedly familiar.

"How was your retreat?" her mother asked.

Dorry couldn't tell her everything over the phone. She settled for, "Fine. How do you feel?"

"I've felt better. But I'm okay."

Dorry wrapped and unwrapped the telephone cord around her finger, trying to hear behind the words. What if her mother really wasn't okay?

They talked a little longer, then Dorry's mother said, "The nurse is here to pick on me. Come see me tomorrow, all right?"

"I will," Dorry said. She wanted to add "I love you"—she'd said it to near strangers over and over again during the weekend—but somehow the words wouldn't come out right for her own mother.

Once she hung up, Dorry was fidgety. What were you supposed to do when your mother was in the hospital? She made herself a ham-salad sandwich, but couldn't eat more than two or three bites. She threw it into the garbage disposal and let it run until every shred of the sandwich was annihilated. Her father glared, because the disposal interfered with his TV reception. Dorry went back to her room, but there was nothing to hold her there. It looked like a museum to her Bryden self, a self that now seemed as distant as the people who used the prehistoric tools did in real museums. She was in Indianapolis now. She was saved. And her mother was in the hospital.

The phone rang. Dorry got it. "So how did it go?" Angela's eager voice rushed at her.

"What?" Dorry asked.

"Telling your parents. Did you pray over them like I told you?"

Dorry picked up the phone and pulled it around the

corner. She went into the bathroom and half shut the door for privacy. She sat on the toilet seat. "I didn't—I haven't told them yet." Dorry was going to explain about her mother's heart attack, but the news seemed too new to be shared yet. She had to get used to it before she told anyone else.

"Oh, Dorry." Angela sounded so disappointed, Dorry was afraid she might cry. "You must tell them right away, even if they disapprove. Especially if they disapprove—remember how God loves you more for being persecuted? If you don't tell, the Devil will work on you, crawl in the cracks between your real, Fishers life, and the fake life you show your family. Or, well . . . I don't like to bring this up, but if you won't tell, perhaps it's a sign that you didn't receive a real salvation."

Dorry squinted at the blank white wall in front of her and struggled to make sense of what Angela was saying.

"—Do you feel your salvation was real?" Angela asked.

"Of course." Wasn't it? Dorry stared at the cracks in the tile floor as if they held the answer.

"Well, then—" Angela began slowly, revving up for another flurry of words.

Dorry couldn't bear to have Angela think so poorly of her. "My mother had a heart attack," Dorry blurted out.

"What?"

"Friday, while I was at the retreat. She's in the hospital."

There was a silence at the other end, as if Angela needed time to adjust to Dorry's news. Dorry listened to the phone's static.

"Oh, Dorry, that's awful. How is she?" Angela finally said. Her voice ached with compassion and concern now. Dorry thought it might make her cry.

"She's okay now," Dorry said.

"Oh, Dorry, I feel so bad for you. Do you want me to come over and pray with you?"

Pray—that's what she should have done, she realized belatedly. For a second she longed to have Angela with her, being compassionate and telling her what to do, what to feel.

"Is your father there? We could pray with him, too, give him comfort—"

That clinched it. Dorry couldn't imagine Angela praying with her father. She could picture his skeptical frown already. "No, no, you don't have to come," Dorry said.

"I'll call the prayer chains, though. Did anyone tell you Fishers has twenty different prayer chains? By ten o'clock, your mother will have eighty people praying for her. We'll make sure she gets through this."

I want that, Dorry almost said. Instead, she murmured, "Thanks."

"That's what we're here for," Angela said. "But Dorry, you have to tell at least your father about being saved. Or you won't be."

"I will," Dorry promised.

Angela finished with a prayer over the phone. After she hung up, Dorry continued holding the receiver up to her ear, listening to the dial tone. "God?" she whispered. "Can you make Mom better? Do I have to tell my dad about things?" The phone hummed. Dorry sighed and hung up, not sure why she was acting like God would talk right back. Angela made it sound like that's what He did for her.

Dorry took the phone back to the kitchen. Her dad was still watching TV in the living room. Heart pounding, she went and sat on the couch beside him. "Dad? I was—"

"Can't you wait for the commercial?" he growled.

Obediently, Dorry waited until the actors in police uniforms were replaced by a commercial for Ex-Lax. "I was—I mean, I kind of had a religious experience at the retreat. We were wrong, at Bryden Methodist. I wasn't baptized right. But I was this weekend, so I know I'll go to heaven now—" She knew she wasn't saying things right. At the retreat, Pastor Jim had told of people being saved hearing about someone else's conversion. Dorry thought the way she had started, her story wouldn't save a flea.

Dorry's dad was looking at her the same way he would look at a used-car salesman. "What do you mean, you weren't baptized right? After your mom spent three weeks on that christening gown you had to wear—"

"But it wasn't my choice, see? I had to consciously, uh, accept Jesus and ask Him into my heart . . . And I had to be dunked, not just sprinkled . . ." Dorry didn't add that it had been in a swimming pool.

Dorry's dad was shaking his head anyway.

"What are you talking about? What church is this?"

"Fishers of Men. It's wonderful." Dorry knew she was supposed to invite him to join, too, to pray with her and assure his own eternal salvation. But she didn't know how to say it, so she just stopped talking.

Her dad's TV show came back on with a burst of sirens and gunfire. He turned back to the TV.

"Look, I've got enough to worry about right now. Don't bother me with this stuff, okay?"

"Okay, Dad," Dorry said obediently. She went back to her room and flopped down on her bed with the home-work she'd neglected all weekend long. She'd done it. She'd told her dad. Angela would be proud. God would be proud.

Dorry just felt foolish.

CHAPTER ELEVEN

THE CALLS BEGAN FIFTEEN minutes later.

"We pray for Reenie Stevens, that God will heal her and cradle her spirit in His arms," the strange voices said over the phone, one after another.

They came at five-minute intervals, as if everyone in Fishers had synchronized their watches and signed up for a certain time.

"Who's that?" Dorry's dad growled after the fifth call, the fifth time Dorry picked up the phone and then said nothing but, "Hello?" and "Thank you. Good-bye."

"Just some people from my, uh, church," Dorry said. "They're praying for Mom."

Dorry's dad grunted. Dorry picked up the phone again. "Hello," she said. "Thank you. Good-bye."

Each call warmed her like a small ember. She didn't

recognize any of the voices, but these people cared about her mother. She was touched that they called. She was touched that someone, probably Angela, had bothered remembering Dorry's mother's name. Dorry must have mentioned it sometime over the weekend.

The phone rang again. "Hello?" she said. ". . . Thank you. Good-bye."

Dorry lost track of the number of calls. She was beginning to feel overwhelmed. On the couch, her father was clearing his throat and coughing in ever-louder expressions of disgust. Finally, in one call where the voice sounded vaguely familiar, there was a pause after Dorry said "Good-bye." Dorry didn't hang up.

"Uh, Dorry? This is Lara. We're not supposed to do anything except pray, but I just wanted you to know how sorry I am."

Dorry hadn't seen much of Lara since the first Fishers party. "Thanks, Lara," Dorry said. She wondered if Lara was still a kleptomaniac, or if she'd reformed again.

Dorry's father was suddenly right behind her. "I don't care if that's God Himself," he said. "You tell those people to quit bothering us."

Dorry felt stung. She was trying to decide what to do when Lara said quietly, "I heard that. I'll tell the others just to pray amongst themselves, not call. See you at school. Bye."

Dorry hung up. She glared angrily at her father, but his back was turned so the effect was lost. She wasn't a good glarer anyway. And under her anger was a little relief. She didn't want to spend the whole night answering the phone either.

Back on the couch, her dad flipped through the TV channels. "We've got to keep the phone lines open, in case there's news from the hospital," he said.

That was the closest he'd come to an apology, Dorry knew. Once when she was about six or seven, he'd accidentally driven his pickup over her pink Barbie bicycle. The way he'd apologized then had been to tell her that he'd never thought the wheels were attached right anyway. But at Christmas there'd been a new bike under the tree.

"You could have told me," Dorry grumbled now. She went back to her homework. The phone didn't ring again.

The next few days Dorry felt like she had two entirely separate lives. Part of the time, she all but lived at the hospital, spending endless hours by her mother's bed. She got used to the nurses constantly interrupting, the automatic blood pressure cuff inflating and deflating on her mother's arm, the trays clattering outside in the hall. It would have been unbearably boring if it hadn't been so terrifying. They kept a heart monitor on her mother, and Dorry couldn't keep herself from watching it. What if its soothing pulse of green light turned into one long streak? What if its low, steady beeping turned into a sudden, high-pitched screech? Dorry had seen that happen thousands of times on TV. She knew what it looked like when people died. It was always a relief to walk out of the room, out of sight of the monitor. Yet Dorry clutched an almost superstitious belief that as long as she watched, the monitor and her mother's heart would go on as usual. So she never wanted to leave.

In her other life, Dorry barely thought about her mother. She answered people's questions automatically, as briefly as possible. In her other life, she was a Fisher.

"You're doing so well," Angela raved at lunch on Tuesday. It was just the two of them, because Dorry was having her first discipling session. "I can tell you're going to be one of the best new Fishers."

Dorry squinted at Angela. All she'd done was correctly answer a list of test questions: Who is your savior? Why did you need to be saved? Angela had given her the questions and answers to memorize the day before. It was no different than memorizing the Bill of Rights for American history.

"Maybe you'll even be ready for an E Team soon," Angela said.

"A what?"

"I'll explain some other time. We have too much to

do today." Angela took out a sheet of paper. "How much time have you spent praying since yesterday?"

Dorry thought back. She'd gone straight from school to the hospital, and stayed there until visiting hours ended. Then she'd gone home and studied, because she had an algebra test. She had done her bedtime prayers the way Angela had told her, only quicker. But she'd slept too late to pray in the morning.

"Ten minutes," she said, though it had probably been only five.

"Oh, Dorry." Angela let out a great sigh of disappointment and put her pen down. "You need to pray at least an hour every day. How can you expect God to give you the time of day in heaven if you won't even give him one twenty-fourth of your time on earth?"

Dorry thought that sounded like a Pastor Jim line. It worked. She felt guilty.

"Maybe it was fifteen minutes," she said. "I had that algebra test, and then with my mom in the hospital—" She wanted to say she'd sort of been praying in the hospital, hoping so fervently that her mother would get well. But she didn't think

Angela would count that.

"Dorry, Dorry, Dorry." Angela was shaking her head. "Do you believe that algebra is more important than God?"

"Of course not. But—"

"And I'm not saying you shouldn't visit your mother in the hospital, but you know Jesus did say, 'He who loves father or mother more than me is not worthy of me.' Matthew 11:37. Dorry, Fishers has to be the most important thing in your life." Angela wrote something down on her sheet of paper. "You must pray at least an hour and a half for the next five days to make up for this. Okay?"

Dorry bit her lip, holding back rebellious words—Who died and left you in charge? What right do you have to tell me what to do?—but she knew the answers. She'd just repeated them for Angela. Jesus had died. Angela was her discipler. Angela knew what Dorry had to do.

"Okay," Dorry said.

"Good!" Angela rewarded her with a smile so radiant it could have been an angel's. Then she turned back to her paper. "Now, what sins have you committed?"

"What?" Dorry said.

"What sins have you committed?" Angela asked again. She spoke slowly, as if Dorry was a foreigner who had trouble understanding English. She tapped her pen on the paper. "We have to keep track of your progress as a Fisher, and one way to do that is for me to write down all of your sins at every discipling session. I give a number to each sin depending on how bad it is, and then we can see how your numbers go down as you become more faithful."

"Like grades," Dorry said.

"Sort of."

"Don't I get any credit for doing good things, too?"

"Of course." Angela nodded. "You're expected to do virtuous acts, especially for unbelievers, so they see the error of their ways. But first—you have to tell me your sins."

Dorry looked around. They were smack in the middle of the cafeteria, with other kids on either side. She'd noticed them sneaking strange looks at Dorry and Angela as it was. "Here? Can't we go somewhere more private?"

Angela looked to her right and to her left, as if noticing for the first time that they weren't alone. "God's opinion of you is the only one that matters," she said, then shrugged. "But you're new. We can move, if you want."

They shifted to a section of table with several empty chairs on each side. Dorry felt like confessing quickly, before anyone else sat near them, but she hesitated again. "Who else sees what you write down?" she asked. She didn't want Brad knowing all the bad things about her.

"Is that what you're worried about?" Angela asked, with a ripple of laughter. "Oh, Dorry, I thought you trusted me more than that."

Dorry remembered that she hadn't really let herself fall during the trust exercise. But that was before she was saved.

"I promise you," Angela said. "Your secrets are safe with me."

"Like Catholics having private confession?"

"You can think of it like that," Angela said.

Dorry looked into Angela's perfect blue eyes, and still hesitated. What counted as sin? If she had, say, picked her nose, would she have to confess that? She'd never tell Angela something like that. Never.

"Let me help you," Angela said. She took out a new piece of paper and wrote "Categories of sins" in bold, looping letters at the top. Then, down the side, she wrote: "Pride, greed, sloth, selfisŸess, sins of the flesh, disobedience of God's will, worship of false gods."

"Look at these and tell me what you've done. I'll write down 'disobedience,' because you didn't pray enough, and 'worship of false gods,' because you cared more about algebra than God."

Dorry wanted to protest—she had hardly been worshiping algebra. But Angela was already saying, conciliatorily, "I'm sure you'll do better next time. Remember, I'm not judging you, I'm just keeping track. For your own information. What else?"

Dorry gulped. "Well, I don't know where you'd put it, but I didn't do a very good job of telling my parents about being a Fisher," she admitted. After the disaster with her dad, she'd only told her mother, "I went ahead and joined this new church." Then a nurse had come in to check her mother's medication and, somehow, when the nurse was gone again, the conversation went off in a different direction.

"But you did tell them?" Angela asked, her pen hovering over the paper.

"Ye-es," Dorry said.

"Well," Angela said forgivingly, "that's the first step. You should be witnessing to them constantly, so you'll do better there. I won't write anything down."

Dorry felt guiltier that Angela hadn't judged her guilty. She looked back at the list. "SelfisŸess," she said. "I've been selfish. In the hospital, when I should be concerned about my mother, I just keep thinking about myself, how awful it would be for me if she died."

Angela nodded approvingly, as if relieved that Dorry recognized how bad she was. She wrote on her paper, and Dorry felt a strange mixture of pride and shame that *that* sin was worth recording.

Her eyes traveled down the list. She felt compelled to come up with more sins. "Maybe this is sins of the flesh," she said. "Or maybe not. But I kind of have a crush on Brad." She kept her head lowered. She couldn't look at Angela, confessing that. "And at the same time, there was this one guy, Zachary, at the retreat, that I was kind of interested in. Is it wrong to be attracted to two guys at once?"

Angela tilted her head, thinking. "Yes," she said. "Usually. It can be a sin to be attracted to just one, if you're lusting after him. Do you feel lust for Brad?"

Dorry couldn't look up. Her face burned. Why had she said that? "Maybe," she whispered.

Angela patted her on the back. "That's okay," she said. "In Fishers, we try to remove a lot of that temptation. Boys and girls are kept separate in many of our activities, especially the ones for new Fishers who are more likely to be troubled by sexual feelings."

"Oh," Dorry said. "So no one's allowed to date?" She was embarrassed by the whole subject. What if Angela laughed and said, "What? You think someone would want to date you?" But Angela shook her head and answered seriously, "Of course people are allowed to date. But only the Fishers who are more mature in their faith are encouraged to. You must be secure in your relationship with God before seeking anything else."

Angela wrote something down on her paper. Dorry pretended to be intent on the list of sin categories. She had to say something else. She grabbed on to the next sin she could find. "I guess this counts as greed," she began. "Now that my mom is sick and can't work for a while, we have to really watch our money, and that bothers me. I don't think its fair."

As soon as she'd said it, Dorry felt ashamed again. How could she tell that to Angela—Angela, who owned a sports car, whose father drove a Mercedes? She reminded herself what Angela had said about not judging her friends by money. And in her short time in Fishers, she'd already heard a lot about Jesus' wealth being entirely spiritual.

Angela lowered her pen, Dorry's sins of the flesh forgotten. "Are things really bad?" Angela asked compassionately.

"Not really, really bad, but—oh, I guess so. My dad said I should get a job myself if I want to save any more for college."

Dorry didn't explain the rest. It wasn't really the idea of working that bothered her—she didn't think it'd be that hard to flip hamburgers or run a cash register. But even with the confidence of being a Fisher, she still dreaded the thought of going into stores and restaurants and having to ask for applications or an interview or whatever you had to do. Applying for a job wouldn't have been that bad in Bryden, where she knew the guy who managed Wendy's and she'd gone to school with the kids of the woman who ran K-Mart. But Indianapolis was overwhelming enough without thinking about searching for a job.

Angela chewed thoughtfully on the end of her pen.

"Let me talk to some other Fishers," she said. "I'm sure we can find you something."

Dorry blinked and leaned toward Angela. "Really?"

"Sure." Angela made another note on her paper. "Anything else?"

A thousand potential, small sins flitted through Dorry's mind, but they all seemed more embarrassing than sinful. "No," she said.

Angela looked at her watch. The lunch period was almost over, and the tables around them were clearing out. "We'll have the next discipling session on Saturday, right before Bible Study."

"Bible Study?"

"Didn't I tell you? You're ready for that now. You'll go into a Saturday afternoon session, to start with."

"Don't I get a choice?"

"Well, sure, but I know all the Bible Study groups, and I know this one is best for you." Angela's voice held a slight note of impatience, as if Dorry shouldn't have questioned her.

"Okay," Dorry said obediently.

"Now lets pray together," Angela said.

Dorry looked around, hoping no one was watching, before tardily bowing her head. Angela was already praying. Dorry only half listened, because she was trying to figure out what to say when Angela's smooth flow of words stopped and it was Dorry's turn. She wanted to pray for forgiveness, for resenting the way Angela took charge of everything, but she couldn't say that in front of Angela. And, Dorry reminded herself, Angela was going to get her a job. She was only trying to help. She knew a lot more than Dorry did about being a Fisher.

CHAPTER TWELVE

TWO DAYS LATER, DORRY stood on a wide brick porch and tentatively lifted and dropped a heavy brass knocker. It thudded gracelessly against the door.

"Nervous?" Angela said beside her.

"Sort of," Dorry said. "I mean, I've babysat before, so I know I can do the job. But I'm not really good at meeting new people."

"You'll do fine," Angela said.

They were in one of the nicest neighborhoods in the city—at least it looked nice to Dorry. All the houses were big and widely spaced, with generous yards and large trees. Someone from Fishers—Dorry wasn't sure exactly who—lived one street over, and knew that the woman who lived here, a Mrs. Garringer, needed a babysitter three or four afternoons a week.

"Okay, okay, you can watch, but you have to turn it down," someone was shouting inside as the door opened.

Dorry straightened up and smiled, trying to look presentable. The woman on the other side of the door was young and exotic looking, with short, dark, curly hair and kohl-lined eyes. She was wearing green leggings and a white T-shirt, and had a baby balanced on her right hip. A little girl clung to her left leg, alternately hiding and peeking out. The sound of Big Bird singing the alphabet welled from another room. The woman winced.

"Jasmine, I'm not joking. Turn that down, right now, or I'll turn it off," she yelled.

Big Bird got about a half a decibel softer.

The woman turned back to Dorry and Angela and made a face. "Welcome to the madhouse," she said. "I told the kids they needed to behave, so they wouldn't scare the new babysitter, but that didn't work. Come on in. I'm April Garringer. This fat guy is Seth, and the one pretending to be shy is Zoe. Which one of you is Dorry?"

"I am," Dorry said, as Angela explained, "I'm just a friend who brought her. Just tell me where to sit to be out of the way."

Mrs. Garringer laughed. "If you like *Sesame Street*, the family room is open. If you want to be able to hear yourself think, you can come into the living room with us." She bent down to the little girl. "Zoe, are you sure

117

you don't want to go watch TV with Jasmine?" The little girl shook her head and clung tighter. Mrs. Garringer shrugged. "Okay, but you're going to think this is dull."

Mrs. Garringer led the way into a large, airy room full of what Dorry was sure had to be very expensive furniture: Queen Anne tables, formal couches, stylish lamps. But the effect was ruined by the layers of toys everywhere. Dorry moved a huge stuffed duck to the floor before sitting down.

"I don't clean," Mrs. Garringer explained. "I figure it's a waste of time, since my kids can demolish any room in under two minutes. So don't worry about being expected to pick up after them. Basically I just want someone to play with them. And keep them from killing each other."

"I can do that," Dorry said.

"Good. That's more than I feel capable of, some days." The laugh that accompanied the joke put Dorry at ease. "Let me explain what I'm looking for. In my life before children, I taught art classes at Butler. I had the insane notion that if I quit to be with my kids full-time, I'd have time to work on my own sculpture. Wrong. So after listening to me gripe about it pretty much nonstop, my husband had the brilliant idea that if I got a regular babysitter a couple times a week, and used the time to sculpt, I'd be a lot happier. He thought I should advertise in the paper, put signs up in the library, that kind of thing.

But I didn't want to interview every crazy in the city. So when the Murrins recommended you, I was delighted."

"The Murrins?" Dorry said.

"Yes. They go to your church, right?"

"We're all in Fishers of Men together," Angela said smoothly. "The Murrins are fairly new, so I don't think Dorry knows them well."

Dorry realized suddenly that she didn't know any of the adult Fishers, except Pastor Jim.

Mrs. Garringer was frowning. "I was under the impression that you'd babysat for them."

"No," Dorry said. "I—"

Angela interrupted. "I'm sorry if there was any confusion, but Dorry is still a great babysitter. She took a Red Cross babysitting course when she was twelve, and passed with the highest score in the class. She's certified in infant CPR. And she's taken care of lots of her nieces and nephews all her life."

"That does sound good," Mrs. Garringer said. "But I'd still like some references before you leave today."

"Sure," Dorry said. She was relieved that Angela had listed her qualifications for her—Angela had made them sound more impressive than Dorry would have. But Mrs. Garringer was looking at Dorry like there was something wrong that she couldn't speak for herself.

Zoe inched away from her mother's side and grabbed

the stuffed duck at Dorry's feet. Clutching it tightly, she leaned against Dorry's leg. "Are you going to be our babysitter?" she asked.

"I don't know. It's up to your mom," Dorry said.

Zoe tilted her head first one way, then the other, flipping her hair all the way over. "I hope so. I like you. You've got a big nose just like Grandpa Jack."

"Zoe!" Mrs. Garringer said. "I'm sorry—"

"It's okay," Dorry said. She put her finger gently on Zoe's nose. "And you've got a little nose just like my nephew Jason."

Zoe giggled and ran out of the room. The baby, Seth, gurgled at Dorry.

"Well," Mrs. Garringer said. "It's a good sign if my kids like you. Let me explain the hours. It'd just be Mondays, Wednesdays, and Fridays, from the time school's out until six or six thirty, depending on how things go. Could you do that?"

Dorry nodded.

"And if everything works out, maybe you could babysit a few Friday or Saturday nights, if my husband and I ever get a chance to get away. We've got some weekend babysitters we've used before, but lately it seems like they're never available."

Dorry was about to say, "I can work weekends, too,"

but Angela was already talking for her. "Dorry can't work weekends, because we have a lot of Fishers of Men functions then," Angela said.

Mrs. Garringer turned to Dorry, as if waiting for her to agree. Dorry was too confused to say anything. Why wouldn't Angela let her speak for herself? What would be wrong with missing a Fishers event every now and then? Surely God wouldn't send her to hell for that.

After a minute, Mrs. Garringer shrugged. "Oh, well. It's not like we ever go anywhere anyhow."

From the next room, Zoe shrieked, "Mom-my! Jasmine threw my duck on the table! Get it for me!"

Mrs. Garringer sighed and began shifting the baby so she could get up. He started crying.

"I'll help her," Dorry said quickly. "You stay there."

Mrs. Garringer settled back with a grateful look. Nestled against his mother's shoulder again, the baby was instantly soothed.

Dorry followed the sounds of screams and *Sesame Street*. Zoe started clapping as soon as she stepped into the family room. "It's Dorry!" she said. "Jasmine, that's our new babysitter."

Jasmine looked to be four or five, an elfin girl with long curls.

"I was really bad," she said gravely. "I'm not supposed

to take toys away from Zoe. Are you going to tell Mommy?"

"No," Dorry said. "But don't do it again."

"Okay," Jasmine said.

Dorry retrieved the duck from the top of a Ping-Pong table covered with books and magazines.

"Thank you," Zoe said. "Now I really, *really* like you."

When Dorry got back to the living room, Angela broke off in the middle of a sentence. Both she and Mrs. Garringer looked up at Dorry in a strange way. Dorry wasn't sure what had happened when she was out of the room, but something had changed.

"I was just saying how much you'd like to get this job," Angela said smoothly. "Right?"

"Um, yes," Dorry said.

"Well, everything sounds good to me," Mrs. Garringer said. "And you already seem to have established a rapport with Zoe. I do want to check your references"— she darted a quick glance at Angela. Dorry didn't know why—"but why don't you just plan on starting on Monday? I'll call you to cancel only if someone says you're a convicted axe murderer or something."

Behind the axe murderer joke and Mrs. Garringer's mischievous grin, there was a hint of uncertainty.

"That's fine," Dorry said, doing her best to sound trustworthy. "I'll see you Monday, because I'm not an axe murderer."

"You don't even own an axe, do you, Dorry?" Angela joked.

Everybody laughed, but the laughter was a little strained. Dorry wrote out a list of people she'd babysat for in Bryden, with their phone numbers. They agreed on an hourly rate that sounded ridiculously high to Dorry, but she figured babysitters made more in a big city.

Getting back into Angela's car afterward, Dorry wondered if she should say something about the way Angela had acted, answering questions for Dorry, telling Mrs. Garringer what Dorry could and couldn't do. Angela had acted like she was Dorry's mother, and Dorry was just a little kid who couldn't speak for herself. Dorry shoved her schoolbooks and her Fishers Bible out of the way and sat down. The more she thought about it, the angrier she got. And she needed to be getting calmer, so she wouldn't say anything she didn't mean. Anything unchristian. "I—" she started, and stopped.

Just then Angela slid into the seat beside her and turned and hugged Dorry. "I'm so proud of you," she said, holding Dorry by the shoulders and earnestly peering into her face.

"Why?" Dorry asked, unable to keep a certain harshness out of her voice. "For getting the job?"

"Yeah, sure, for that, but really for something more important."

Dorry frowned. "What?"

"For submitting to authority so obediently."

"Authority?" Dorry said in disbelief.

"Yes," Angela said firmly. "Authority. A lot of new Fishers start viewing their disciplers as busybodies—or worse—whenever their disciplers bring their God-given authority into the new person's life. Its like the Devil is whispering in their ear, 'This is *your* life. Nobody else has the right to make decisions for you. Tell them where to go.' But you—what's the word?—deferred. You didn't argue when I made it clear to Mrs. Garringer that God comes first in your life."

"No. I didn't," Dorry agreed guiltily. She didn't admit that she'd wanted to argue.

"So," Angela said, releasing Dorry's shoulders and turning to the steering wheel. "I'm going to say an extra prayer tonight thanking God for your humility of spirit. Not every discipler is so blessed."

Dorry didn't think that left her anything to say. She sat utterly speechless as Angela drove her to Bible Study. Enormous houses she once would have stared at, mouth agape, flashed by, but she barely saw them. Becoming a Fisher was like learning a new language, she thought. No, it was more than that—when you learned a new language, you were allowed to keep talking the old one, too. Angela seemed to want Dorry to become a totally different person. Dorry remembered a Bible verse they'd talked about at the retreat, something about how once someone was a Christian, he was a new creation. His old self was gone. So it made sense, what Angela was doing.

And what had the old Dorry Stevens been worth, anyway?

CHAPTER THIRTEEN

DORRY'S MOTHER CAME HOME on Sunday, looking pale and thinner and declaring, "I don't want to eat hospital food ever again the rest of my life." And Dorry, helpfully carrying her mother's suitcase in the door, thought grimly, *I hope the rest of your life is a* long *time.* Dorry's father only frowned and snorted. Both of them forgot to tell Dorry's mother about the flowers Angela had sent for her homecoming. When Dorry's mother saw them on the kitchen counter—a grand bouquet of exotic flowers Dorry didn't recognize but knew had to be unbelievably expensive—she flushed and practically went speechless.

"Gene, how could you—" she began. "That must have cost a week's salary, and with me not working. . . ."

"Ain't from me," Dorry's dad said tightly.

Dorry's mom gaped at Dorry. "That babysitting job was supposed to be money for you—"

"Relax, Mom," Dorry said. "My friend Angela sent them. From my church. Wasn't that nice?"

Dorry saw her parents exchange a glance. "Yes. Very nice," her mother said.

But the way she said it made Dorry feel weird about the flowers. They were all wrong in the Stevenses' apartment, crowded on the counter by dirty pots and pans and their old black rotary phone, brought from Bryden. She tried to recapture the thrill she'd felt when the flowers had arrived—the sudden, excited disbelief, the amazement that Angela cared so much about her and her family. But it was gone, replaced by a squeamish discomfort.

"Some people from that church visited me in the hospital this morning, too," Dorry's mother said, sinking onto the couch.

"Really? Some of my friends?" Dorry was surprised.

"It was an older couple. They'd just been sent out to, uh, witness." Dorry's mother said "witness" the way she might mention unpleasant bodily functions.

"But didn't you like them?" Dorry persisted.

"Sure," her mother said, but Dorry could tell that she really didn't. "Gene, can you hand me that remote?"

The TV came on. Dorry knew better than to try to

carry on a religious discussion in the face of a McDonald's commercial.

"I'll do the dishes," she volunteered. If nothing else, she could report it to Angela for her "Virtuous Acts" list. It would be worth double because she had done it for unbelievers. At the sink, up to her elbows in greasy suds, Dorry reminded herself that she was supposed to be thinking of her parents as unbelievers, however strange it seemed. She shouldn't worry about what the Fishers who'd visited her mother had thought of her, or what she thought of them. She should be glad other Fishers were trying to convert her parents, because then it wouldn't be entirely up to her.

"If you don't want your family to go to hell, you must convert them," Angela had said repeatedly. "You know what happens to people who aren't baptized as Fishers. No other church lives the Bible as God commands. Would you be happy in paradise knowing your loved ones were experiencing the worst agonies imaginable for all eternity?"

"No," Dorry had said. Things sounded so simple the way Angela put them. But now . . . Dorry stole a glance back at her parents, still sitting on the couch staring at the TV like nothing else much mattered. Dorry's dad was flipping through the channels, as usual. Dorry had changed and they were the same people they'd always been. Even with her mom's heart attack. Dorry didn't know how she would have survived the whole ordeal without Fishers. But her parents didn't think much of religion, didn't think they needed it, thank you very much. Dorry couldn't imagine anyone being harder to convert than her parents. But she had to try.

"Mom, do you think you and Dad could go to a Fishers service with me some Sunday?" she asked, interrupting yet another commercial.

"Maybe when I'm feeling a little better," her mother said, without looking up.

Dorry sighed. When her mother was feeling better, she'd be back at work, and always too tired or too busy on Sunday mornings. That was how it'd been back in Bryden. Dorry hadn't cared then. But now—why couldn't her parents see the glory she carried around with her all the time now? Why didn't they want that, too? Dorry resolved to act as holy as possible, to let them see what they were missing.

The next few weeks passed quickly. Dorry settled into a routine of babysitting three afternoons a week for the Garringers—her references had checked out, as she knew they would. She couldn't imagine a better job. Dorry had always liked little kids in a vague way—little kids didn't care what you looked like, as long as you played with them. But Dorry quickly decided that the Garringer kids were her all-time favorites.

And as much as Dorry loved them, they seemed to adore her, too. When Jasmine and Zoe started jumping on the couch or throwing crackers on the floor, all Dorry had to say was, "Should I get your mom?" and they'd settle down. Then they'd hug and kiss her and moan, "No, Dorry. We'll be good. We want yo-oou."

As soon as he saw his sisters piling onto Dorry, Seth usually climbed on, too, making kissing motions with his lips. Otherwise, he mainly crawled around the house happily oblivious to his sisters' mania. He never seemed to mind barely missing getting jumped on while he ate the crackers they'd thrown on the floor. At first, Dorry tried to stop him from popping dropped crackers and stray Cheerios and lost Goldfish into his mouth. But Mrs. Garringer, coming into the kitchen for another cup of coffee, had laughed, "Oh, don't worry about that. If he can't eat off the floor, he'll miss out on half his daily diet. A little dirt never hurt anybody. Builds immunities."

"Okay," Dorry had said uneasily. It did simplify her job.

She still wasn't quite comfortable with Mrs. Garringer. Maybe it was because they'd gotten off on the wrong foot, with Angela doing all the talking for Dorry that first day. Dorry could be playing with the kids, having a great time jumping up and down in an out-of-control game of Simon Says, when Mrs. Garringer would walk in and announce, "Okay, I've made enough of a mess for the day.

Want to relax and have a Coke with me until it's time for you to go?" And suddenly Dorry would feel totally foolish and self-conscious. At first, Mrs. Garringer asked her about school and her friends and her life, because, Mrs. Garringer said, "I'm in a mommy ghetto where most of the people I know have diapers and formula on the brain. I can't remember—what's life like without kids?"

Dorry was sure Mrs. Garringer's life had been glamorous and exciting before her kids were born. Dorry stammered and blushed trying to explain what she did— Fishers parties and Fishers services and Fishers studies.

"Sounds like you're very involved in your church," Mrs. Garringer had said. "Don't you miss being around people with more diverse views?"

Dorry didn't know how to answer that. She was glad she didn't have to because Zoe interrupted just then, scrambling into her lap and insisting, "Read to me, read to me, READ TO ME!"

When Dorry described her discomfort later to Angela, Angela shook her head in disbelief. "Dorry, don't you see what an opportunity you missed? She was practically begging for you to witness to her. If that family ends up in hell, it will be your fault."

Dorry had apologized and watched Angela total up an all-time high number for her sin category—missing an opportunity to witness was counted as one of the worst possible disobediences to God's will. But she didn't feel as guilty as she knew she ought to. The Garringers didn't seem to need religion. They were perfect the way they were. Even though Dorry had already sat through plenty of sermons on the text, "All have sinned and fall short of the glory of God"—and nodded solemnly with everyone else, and said "Amen" with everyone else, and believed fervently with everyone else—she still couldn't make herself worry about the Garringers going to hell.

Actually, she was too busy to worry about much of anything. There were always tests and papers at school—the work was definitely harder than it had ever been at Bryden High School, and the good grades that had come automatically back in Bryden were now hard earned, fought for. But Dorry was proud that some of her teachers were starting to notice how hard she was working.

Most of that work was late at night, long after her parents had turned off the TV and gone to bed, because between babysitting and Fishers, she almost never had any other time. Bible Study was now twice a week, on Tuesday and Saturday. There were services on Wednesday night and Sunday morning, song vigil Sunday night, and Fishers parties or funfests most Friday and Saturday nights. Angela moved her discipling sessions to Tuesday and Thursday after school, and before Bible Study on

Saturday. And her Bible Study group hung out together almost every other spare moment.

"To think I was afraid you'd be lonely when I went back to work," Dorry's mother said wistfully one Friday night when Dorry's Bible Study group showed up to take her out for pizza, leaving her mother home alone. "You're getting so popular—"

"Popular's not the way to think about it," Dorry replied. "God loves me. That's what matters. My fellow Fishers just embody that love."

It was true—with the other girls, Dorry always felt loved and accepted. The familiar greeting, "Hey, Chocolate!" always sounded like a blessing after her weeks of loneliness. It was so cozy to be with a group of friends who all agreed on everything. She remembered the arguments she'd had from time to time with her friends back in Bryden—one time she'd gotten mad at Marissa for saying Joe Hanley wasn't cute, when Dorry thought he was the biggest hunk in town. She'd been so shallow then. Her Bible Study friends mainly talked about Fishers and the Bible, even on Friday nights over pizza, even at lunch at school, regardless of the stares they got. There were always a few disciplers with them who knew all the answers—if Angela was away, at least one of the other girls' disciplers would be with them. So there wasn't any way they could start fighting about what Jesus meant when he said there was only one door to the kingdom of heaven, or about whether the Creation had really happened. If someone started to disagree, Angela or another discipler would say, "What Bible verse are you referring to?"

Usually the person was trying to bring up something outside the Bible, something secular. Angela in particular had an amazing way of looking the person right in the eye, patting her hand, and saying, "The Devil is leading you astray. You know there is only one Word of God, only one book we can believe absolutely."

And that would end the argument. Dorry was always stunned by Angela's quiet authority. How could Angela silence eight girls instantly without even raising her voice? What would it be like to have your words carry such weight? Sometimes Dorry believed she saw the power of God every time she watched Angela.

Dorry never disagreed about anything. She was still feeling her way through the Bible, learning what she was supposed to think.

CHAPTER FOURTEEN

DORRY AND ANGELA SAT on a park bench, the tally sheet of Dorry's sins and virtuous acts between them. Dorry's numbers were good—she'd had no sins to speak of and had stayed late after a Fishers meeting to help one of the freshman members with algebra. She'd even prayed an extra half hour the day before.

Now the discipling session was almost over and for once Angela was pausing to chitchat before the long prayer at the end. Angela had decided to meet in the park today because they were having freakishly warm weather for November. Most of the leaves were off the trees, but the grass was still a lush green. Dorry felt a burst of giddy joy that would have fit more with spring than with autumn.

"You know what today is? Your one-month anniversary

of being saved and joining Fishers," Angela said lazily.

"It is?" Dorry asked, warmed by the thought that Angela had kept track, even if Dorry hadn't.

"Yes. Do you feel you've received the abundant riches of God's love promised at your baptism?"

"Of course," Dorry said. And she did. Her life was so happy now. Thanks to Fishers, she always had friends to be with, and she was right with God. Outside of Fishers, both school and her job were going well. And, best of all, her mother's last doctor's appointment had shown that everything looked good. She was already back at work.

At Bible Study, the other girls had agreed: God had answered the Fishers' prayers for Dorry's mother. Now if only she and Dorry's father could be saved . . . Dorry pushed the thought away, not wanting any problem to disturb her joyful mood.

Angela nodded slowly, her hair bouncing against the park bench. "I thought you'd say things were going well. But you realize what's coming up, don't you? With Thanksgiving?"

Dorry blinked. "We're going home. I told you that," she said. Because her mother's heart attack had thrown everyone off kilter, this would be her family's first trip back to Bryden since August. Dorry had been looking forward to Thanksgiving for weeks. It would be so much fun seeing all her old friends. And she'd always loved

Thanksgiving food—turkey, stuffing, mashed potatoes, Aunt Emma's candied yams. . . . Dorry forced her attention back to Angela. "What do you mean?"

"This will be your first time away from your Fishers brothers and sisters. It will be a test of your faith to spend four days entirely among strangers and unbelievers."

Dorry was about to protest that she would hardly be among strangers, but she knew what Angela meant.

"Do you know how hard it is to pray two hours a day when you have no one to pray with you? When your voice is the only one crying out in the wilderness against blasphemous words and deeds?"

"You make my family sound like a bunch of—" Dorry searched for the right word. Sinners? Heathens? Of course, according to Fishers, they were.

Angela waited. When Dorry didn't finish, she went on. "I'm sure God will be with you and you will pass this test," Angela said. "But you must steel yourself to be strong in your faith, even if all around you are doubters. You remember the verses about preparing yourself for battle against evil?"

"Ephesians 6:14–18," Dorry quoted obediently. "'Stand, therefore, having girded your loins with truth, and having put on the breastplate of righteousness, and having shod your feet with the equipment of the gospel of peace; above all taking the shield of faith, with which you can quench all the flaming darts of the evil one.'" They'd memorized the verse in Bible Study only the week before.

"Exactly," Angela said. "You must see this as a battle. The Devil will be watching for you to slip. He will be there to attack you if you fall."

Dorry looked out across the park. With the blue sky, the warm weather, and her feelings of contentment, she had trouble thinking about the Devil even existing. As for any coming battle with him at Thanksgiving—what was he going to do? Hide behind Aunt Emma's candied yams?

"Here's what you must do," Angela said. "You must pray and read the Bible at least two hours every day. I'll give you a list of verses to study. And call me every night at eight o'clock. We'll do our discipling sessions over the phone."

"But it's long distance," Dorry said. Angela gave Dorry a look that silenced her immediately. If Angela said she had to call, she had to call. She didn't want to protest and have her sin number go up on the tally sheet. "Okay. But why every day?"

"You'll need it," Angela said. "Because now that you've been in Fishers a month, you're ready for the second level of discipling. Congratulations." She threw her arms around Dorry and squeezed. Dorry thought of beauty contestants hugging, acting equally thrilled that one of them was going to be Miss America.

"Well, thanks," Dorry said. "What does that mean?"

"You haven't heard of anyone referred to as a Level Two Fisher?"

Dorry shook her head.

"Oh, good," Angela said. "There were problems before, with people finding out things before they were ready . . . Anyhow, it's kind of like saying you're not a baby Fisher anymore. You're ready for more advanced service to God."

She suddenly raised her arm and waved over her head. Dorry turned and saw several of the girls from her Bible Study scrambling out of a car in the parking lot. When they got closer, Dorry saw that it was only the ones who were disciplers: Sarah, Jamie, Holly, and Tina. Tina was carrying a white box.

"Hey, Chocolate!" some of them yelled across the park. Dorry warmed at the familiar nickname.

"Congratulations, Dorry and Angela! You're the first!" Sarah said when they got close. "But as soon as I get Caitlin to stop swearing, we'll be next."

"No, no, it'll be Terry and me," Holly said. "Except for that one relapse, she hasn't had a beer in a week. Her other sin numbers are coming down, too."

Confused, Dorry turned to Angela. "I thought all that was private," she said.

"Oh, no, once you're Level Two, it's okay," Angela

said with a shrug. "You're allowed to know anything from anyone's discipling session, as long as they're on the same level or lower."

Dorry thought of all the embarrassing things she'd confessed to Angela. She didn't want to ruin the celebration, but she couldn't stop herself from protesting: "But you said—"

"What I said was that you don't have to worry about anyone finding out your secrets," Angela said, almost icily. "And you don't, because everyone who's a Level Two or higher is a Fisher in good standing, who would never hurt you in any way. We all trust each other, right?"

The other girls nodded vigorously. Their bobbing heads reminded Dorry of the toy dogs on springs that had been all the rage for a while in car windows back in Bryden. They wouldn't stop. They were waiting for her to join in. Reluctantly, Dorry nodded, too. None of them cared about sharing secrets. If she admitted how much it bothered her, they'd think she wasn't a good-enough Fisher.

"Good," Angela said. "Now, how about showing Dorry what's in that box?"

"Ta da!" Tina opened the lid. Everyone oohed and aahed. Inside was a cake, beautifully decorated, with the words "Congrats, Dorry" looping across the top in orange icing.

"It's chocolate, of course," Tina said, patting Dorry's arm. "You made my choice easy."

Everyone laughed.

Tina had brought a plastic knife and napkins but no forks, so they ate with their fingers. The chocolate icing smeared on their faces and hands. Dorry had two pieces of the rich, dark cake—a preview, she thought, of all the good food at Thanksgiving.

"Okay, where's the gift?" Jamie squealed when they'd all finished and cleaned up.

"You like to rush things, don't you?" Angela asked. But with a dramatic flourish, she reached into her purse and pulled out a small box wrapped in gold paper and tied with a luminous bow.

"Ooh," some of the girls breathed. They settled into a circle on the ground at Dorry's and Angela's feet. Dorry felt her heart thumping fast, the way it had at the school honors assembly last year, when she'd thought she might get the sophomore highest-grades award, but wasn't sure.

Angela presented the gift to Dorry. Dorry had never held anything so elegant looking.

"You're supposed to open it," someone reminded her.

Hesitantly, Dorry unstuck the bow and eased the tape off the back of the package. This wasn't the way she usually unwrapped presents—she was more likely to rip paper off as quickly as possible. But she didn't want to spoil this.

The paper yielded to a plain white cube. Inside, Dorry found a smaller velvet box. She lifted the hinged lid and gasped. It was a ring, a gold ring embedded with what looked to be small diamonds.

"I can't take this," she protested. "It's too nice."

"It is only a small, inadequate token of the vastness of God's love for you," Angela said, as formally as if reciting a Bible verse. "No one is worthy of His love, but He gives it freely to all who believe and act accordingly. You will wear this always, to be a constant reminder of God's love, of your unworthiness, and of your duty to obey His will."

Gently, Angela eased the ring out of the box and onto the ring finger of Dorry's left hand. It stuck above the knuckle. Without a pause, Angela slipped the ring onto Dorry's pinky instead.

Dorry waffled between embarrassment that her finger was too fat and relief that she wouldn't have to wear the ring where a wedding ring would go. Wasn't there some superstition that if you wore a ring on your wedding finger, you'd never get married? Looking around, Dorry noticed for the first time that all the girls were wearing rings on their left hands.

"The vows?" Tina reminded softly.

Angela put her hand over Dorry's. "Repeat after me. I vow—"

"I vow," Dorry said.

The rest of the words came in groups of two or three, so Dorry had no time to think about what she was vowing. She only put it all together later: "—to be worthy of my discipler's faith in me. I vow to obey her commands unquestioningly. I vow to be a fit servant of God."

"Very good," Angela said when Dorry was done.

One by one, the other girls put their hand on Dorry's and prayed over her. Each ended, "May it be your will, oh Lord. Amen."

"And now the commission," Angela said. "When I was assigned as your discipler, I had to make a list of goals for you at every level. The goals are pretty much the same for everyone at Level One. But at Level Two, I have a lot more choices, because this is an even greater time of coming to accept your discipler's authority."

"How many levels are there?" Dorry asked.

The girls exchanged glances.

"That doesn't matter," Angela said.

"What are all of you?"

The others shared another look that left Dorry out.

"You're not allowed to ask that," Angela said.

"What?"

Angela gave Dorry a look that made her remember

the "unquestioning" part of the vow she'd just made. "No one's allowed to ask higher-level Fishers their numbers. It's like—questioning their authority. Like, if you're a two, you might not listen to a three if you knew she just was a three."

"I see," Dorry said, though she didn't.

Angela stood up and placed her hand on Dorry's shoulders. Her stance reminded Dorry of a queen bestowing knighthood on a subject. "As your discipler, Dorry Stevens, I command you to end your worship of the false god of food. Your body is a temple of God, and you should keep it holy. As a sign that you have turned away from your former evil ways, you shall fast on Thanksgiving Day."

Dorry jerked back. "What? I don't worship food."

Angela shook her head and glared. She put her hands back on Dorry's shoulders. "Furthermore, you shall begin your mission as a witness for God's righteousness. You will join an evangelism team, and you will convert at least one person on your trip to Ohio."

Dorry held back words she knew would get her in trouble.

"In the name of God, Amen," Angela finished.

"Amen," the other girls said.

Tardily, Dorry added, "Amen."

All the girls took turns hugging her again. They acted as though Angela's commands were absolutely ordinary. But Dorry's mind was in turmoil. How could Angela think she worshiped food? She liked it, sure, but who didn't? So she was a little overweight—it was genetic. All the Stevenses were heavyset. And how could she fast on Thanksgiving? What would her family say? As for converting someone in Ohio—she'd been talking to her parents for a month about Fishers, and they were no closer to a conversion than ever. How was she supposed to convert someone in only four days?

But at the back of her mind, a small, guilty voice whispered: *You do eat too much. That's why you're fat. You don't really expect a beautiful, skinny person like Angela to want to be seen with you, do you? She's probably been disgusted by you since she met you. She was just too nice to say so. And you're a coward, too. Angela knows you haven't tried hard enough to convert your parents or anybody else.*

The others were cleaning up and getting ready to go. Tina slid the crumbling remains of the cake back into its bakery box. Before, Dorry would have been tempted to say, "Hey, I'll finish that off. It's not enough to take home." But now the sight of the cake, the heavy feel of it in her stomach, made Dorry feel sick. She watched

Tina carelessly heave the cake box into the trash. She thought of the nickname everyone had called her: Chocolate. Her favorite food. But if Angela was worried that Dorry worshiped food, why did Angela let people call her that?

"Angela," Dorry said. "I don't really have to fast on Thanksgiving, do I?"

Angela stopped in the midst of fastening Dorry's sin tally sheet into her binder. "Of course you do. I told you to. I'm your discipler."

The other girls were working in slow motion—listening, but pretending not to. Dorry wished she'd had the sense to wait until it was just her and Angela. But she couldn't stop now.

"I mean, it's impossible not to eat on *Thanksgiving*. I can't do it. My family will think it's really weird. They'll get upset."

Angela snapped the rings of her binder back together. "Jesus upset a lot of people."

"But if they're upset, how can I convert anyone? Anyhow, I can just try, I can't promise that anyone will be converted—"

"Dorry—" Angela slid her binder into her book bag and turned to face Dorry. "No one expects you to do any of this by yourself. God will help you. That should be enough for you. Let's pray about it, shall we?" Angela bowed her head and clasped Dorry's hand. As if on cue, the other girls smoothly flowed from busily cleaning up to holding hands and looking prayerful. Dutifully, Dorry dropped her head.

CHAPTER FIFTEEN

DORRY PLACED THE STEAMING bowl of freshly mashed potatoes on the table, inches from the plate she knew would be her own. Behind her, one of her nephews dove to catch a Nerf football and banged into the table. Gravy sloshed onto the tablecloth.

"Not in the house!" Dorry's sister Denise yelled.

"—so, like, are kids in Indianapolis wearing those peekaboo blouses? I know *you* wouldn't, but I've been trying to tell Mom that everybody does, and if you tell her, maybe she'll let me wear one—" Dorry's thirteen-year-old niece Heidi chattered as she carelessly put the platter of homemade rolls down on the spot of spilled gravy.

Dorry's stomach rumbled. So far she'd said nothing to anyone about fasting or Fishers. It'd been easy enough to skip breakfast without being noticed. That was every man for himself: cereal grabbed hastily from the command headquarters of the Stevens family's Thanksgiving dinner. Dorry figured her mom hadn't stopped to eat breakfast either, in the midst of stuffing the turkey and mixing rolls and grating slaw. But she'd been sampling all morning, licking spoons and testing seasonings. Only moments ago, she'd thrust a spoon dripping with gravy toward Dorry.

"Here, taste this. Should I add more salt?"

Dorry panicked. The spoon might as well be steaming with the fires of hell. She pretended to be busy with the water pitcher. "Ask Heidi. I can never tell."

"Heidi—oh, what am I thinking. Heidi hates gravy. Denise?" Dorry's mom called.

Dorry's hands shook pouring water. She was weak with hunger. Of course, she'd only missed one meal, but with the smells of all the Thanksgiving food reaching for her, it seemed like much more.

Soon Aunt Emma arrived and slid her candied yams onto the table. The kitchen got more crowded. Boisterous kids hid under the table and tugged on the tablecloth, threatening disaster, until someone shooed them away. Dorry felt faint.

Dorry's mom went and whispered to Dorry's dad, sitting in his recliner in the living room. He stood and whistled so loudly the neighbor's dog began barking. It silenced every Stevens. "Grandma says it's all ready. Let's eat!"

There was the usual scramble for chairs. Dorry sat near the kitchen so she could run errands for her mom. Her uncle Ed ended up on one side of her and her sister Denise on the other.

"Some boy give you that ring?" Uncle Ed said. "You going to leave us and marry some city slicker?"

"Dorry's got a boyfriend?" one of her nephews snickered. Even Heidi turned to look.

"No, no," Dorry said, embarrassed. "It was . . . from my church."

"Churches are handing out rings now? Hot dog!" Denise's husband chuckled. "If they'd just hand out the husband to go with them, you'd be all set, Louise."

Louise was one of Dorry's cousins, still unmarried at thirty-eight. She rolled her eyes and turned back to her stuffing.

Dorry looked around at all the familiar faces, the people she'd known all her life. She had to convert one of them by Sunday. "The ring's not about boyfriends or marriage," Dorry said slowly, searching for bravery. "It's a sign of God's love and devotion, and my own unworthiness, and, and . . . my duty to obey."

There was an awkward silence. Dorry's words seemed

150

to lie on the table as embarrassing and unwanted as the spinach casserole someone brought to Thanksgiving one year during a short-lived health kick.

Then one of the youngest Stevenses called out, "Where's my mac'roni cheese?" and his mother tried to explain there wasn't any. The usual chatter sprang up again. Dorry began passing food. Each dish seemed more desirable than the last: potatoes, rolls, Denise's special cheese-stuffed mushrooms. Dorry dreaded the moment when someone noticed none of it was ending up on her plate. Maybe they wouldn't. Maybe they'd just think she'd eaten quickly and cleanly.

No such luck.

"That church of yours forbids you to eat, too?" Denise asked, between forkfuls of potatoes.

"Just today," Dorry said miserably, her eyes following Denise's fork to her mouth. Mmm. Mashed potatoes. What if Dorry ate just them? How could God mind that? No one would have to know. Resolutely, she shook the thought away. Her stomach growled. "I'm fasting today. It's—like a test."

Denise practically dropped her fork. "What? That's crazy. . ."

Across the table, Dorry's mom instantly stopped comparing grocery prices with Aunt Emma, as if her motherly antenna had just intercepted news of a plane crash. "Oh, honey," she cried. "You didn't tell us that. That can't be right. Surely you misunderstood—"

Dorry shook her head no. She'd understood.

Uncle Ed dug his elbow in her side. "If I was you, I'd tell that church where to go," he said, then guffawed at his own wit.

"What's God got against food?" Aunt Emma asked.

"So you don't eat. What's that do?" Denise asked. She waved her fork so close to Dorry's face that Dorry could easily have leaned forward and gobbled a big bite of potatoes. She swallowed hard.

"If I succeed, it'd be a sign, I mean, proof, that food isn't a false god for me, that I don't care more about it than I do about God and Fishers, the church I'm in—"

Dorry could tell how she sounded by the looks on her family's faces. She stopped.

"Tell you what I'd do," Aunt Emma said suddenly. She stood up, her chair scraping back loudly on the hardwood floor. She dug a spoon deep into her candied yams and, leaning across the table, deposited them on Dorry's plate. Dots of the brown-sugar sauce dribbled across the tablecloth. Then Aunt Emma looked around wildly, eyes lighting on the platter of rolls. She took one and tossed it onto Dorry's plate. She might have gone on, but the other food was out of her reach. "What I'd do," she said, sitting back down, "is I'd eat all I wanted and tell that church I'd follow all their stupid rules tomorrow. If I felt like it. Tell them today's a holiday. It's Thanksgiving. The point of Thanksgiving is to eat."

Dorry gulped. "The point of Thanksgiving is to give thanks to God," she said in a near whisper.

Across the table, her mother frowned, her expression telegraphing the message, "Eat. Now. Quit making a disturbance."

Dorry looked down at her plate, at the hot, yeasty roll, at the succulent candied yams, their pool of brown-sugar sauce spreading across her plate. She could feel everyone staring, waiting to see if she would eat. The food all but called out to her. She felt light-headed. How easy it would be just to pick up the roll. How much she longed to eat. Her stomach twisted. She brought her hand toward the table. She remembered her lazy, joking thought the week before: *What was the Devil going to do? Hide behind Aunt Emma's candied yams?*

Dorry pushed herself away from the table and ran to the stairs.

Behind her she heard several people call, "Dorry!"

"Honestly—" Aunt Emma rumbled.

Dorry could hear more than one chair being pushed back from the table. Who would come after her? Then her father's voice boomed: "Let her go. She'll come back when she gets hungry. No use letting anyone else's food go cold over this."

Crying, Dorry ran to her room, slammed the door, and flung herself across the ancient twin bed brought down from the attic because her own bed was in Indianapolis. It creaked, protesting her weight. Even her bed was against her. Why did everything have to be so hard? How could she stand being so hungry?

"Dear God," she started praying. But her family's mockery—"What's God got against food?"—was too fresh in her ears. She felt more foolish than holy. Maybe Aunt Emma was right. Maybe she shouldn't have to follow rules on a holiday.

After a few moments, Dorry crept out of her room and down the hall to her parents' bedroom. She took the phone from their nightstand and punched in Angela's number. It rang six times before an unfamiliar female voice—Angela's mother? A maid?—answered.

"May I please speak to Angela?" Dorry asked.

"She's eating Thanksgiving dinner and cannot be disturbed," the woman said disapprovingly. "I suggest you call back later."

Dorry went back to her room and sobbed. Oh, Angela couldn't be disturbed because *she* was eating Thanksgiving dinner. Why did she get to eat if Dorry couldn't?

After a while, the knocks started on her door. "Dorry, we're all having pumpkin pie now . . ." "Dorry, we're putting the leftovers away. Don't you want anything?" "Dorry, the relatives are leaving. Don't you want to say good-bye?" She mumbled, "Leave me alone," each time.

Later, when she thought her parents were napping, Dorry crept down the stairs and filled a plate with leftovers. She was too angry to be hungry anymore, but if Angela could eat, so could she. She wolfed down a huge slice of turkey, three rolls, a mound of cold potatoes, and a pile of stuffing laced with visibly congealed butter before her mother came into the kitchen and caught her.

"Dorry—" she began.

Dorry put down the plate and ran back upstairs without speaking.

CHAPTER SIXTEEN

DORRY WOKE TO HEAR the phone ringing, insistently, many times.

Then it stopped and, "Dorry?" her mother called.

Confused about where she was—Indianapolis? No, her old room, with the wrong furniture—she ran into the wall trying to find the door. She squinted at the digital clock. Eleven thirty. Late.

Dorry got the phone downstairs and shouted up, "Got it." She waited to hear the click to be sure her mother had hung up before she said, "Hello?"

"You didn't call," Angela's voice rushed at her. "I was worried about you."

Dorry's stomach churned. She could picture cold potatoes and greasy stuffing and rolls fighting for room inside. "I tried calling earlier. You were eating."

Without entirely intending it, Dorry made the word "eating" an accusation. She wanted to yell so much more—*Why did you ruin my Thanksgiving? I'd been looking forward to this day for months, and now it's over and my family thinks I'm crazy and I barely left my room. And you were eating!*

"You could have called back." Angela's voice was gentle. "Did you have a happy Thanksgiving?"

"Of course not," Dorry sputtered. "You told me to fast, remember?"

"But I always feel so light and holy when I fast. Closer to God. You did fast, didn't you?"

"Yes. I mean—sort of. Just not the whole day."

"Oh, Dorry." Dorry could hear the full weight of Angela's disappointment in her voice. She could picture Angela's exact expression.

"I didn't eat Thanksgiving dinner with my family," Dorry said. "I—I stood up against their persecution, just like in the Bible. But then I called you, and you were eating *your* Thanksgiving dinner, so I had a little to eat later—"

"Oh, Dorry. What sin you fell into. You let the Devil win."

"But *you* ate. It's not fair." Dorry knew she sounded like a sulky child. She didn't care.

"My discipler did not order me to fast," Angela said

157

sternly. "I do not worship the false god of food. So it didn't matter if I ate or not. But you—you promised me. You promised God."

"I'm sorry," Dorry said automatically.

Angela sighed and Dorry felt truly guilty. She had agreed to fast, even if she hadn't wanted to. She should just be more careful from now on about what she agreed to.

"I'm really sorry," she said. "I did the thing that was hardest, not eating with my family. You should have heard what they said." She described the dinner and her dramatic departure from the table. Somehow, telling Angela about it, Dorry almost began to see it the way she wanted Angela to. She wasn't crazy, the way her family saw her. She was holy and pure and strong in her faith. She'd been resolute in the face of ridicule.

"But you ate after that," Angela said softly. Her tone implied that Dorry was weak and contemptible, but might be forgiven.

"Yes. I did," Dorry admitted. She didn't say how much. "But I—I can fast again tomorrow. I can do it the whole day. You'll see." Dorry couldn't believe what she was saying. What if Angela said, "Yes, fast tomorrow"?

But Angela breathed slowly, "No-oo. We'll try that another time. You need to concentrate on your second goal."

In her anguish over fasting, Dorry had forgotten about that. "Converting someone," she said.

"Yes. Whose soul will you save first?"

Dorry thought hard. She didn't want to do this. But if she said, "I can't," Angela would think she was a bad Fisher. So would God. "Maybe my friend Marissa," Dorry said. "I'm going to spend all day with her tomorrow."

"Then I'll pray for her. And you."

They stayed on the phone a lot longer, Angela praying at length over Dorry's sins and her plans for converting Marissa. By the end, hanging up, Dorry almost felt at peace. She worried about Marissa, but Angela had said she should leave those worries to God.

Dorry stood up and raised and lowered her shoulders, sore from sitting with the phone for more than an hour.

"Dorry?"

It was her mother, standing at the foot of the stairs.

"Was that your friend from that church?"

"Yes. Everything's okay now."

Dorry's mother frowned, and Dorry could see the heavy lines of age in her sagging face. She looked so tired. Guiltily, Dorry wondered if it had been good for her to work so hard fixing the Thanksgiving dinner, even though she'd said she wanted to. And then Dorry hadn't even helped her clean up. Wasn't that a sin, too?

"I'm not—" Dorry's mother stopped and began again. "I know you're almost an adult, and certainly there's nothing wrong with religion. We're all Christians, of course.

But this church isn't right for you. They expect too much. They're—unreasonable."

"But Mom—" Dorry reminded herself that she was supposed to be representing Jesus to an unbeliever. It wasn't just her talking to her mom. "God expects a lot of His people. And He gives a lot in return. You should commit yourself wholly to Him, too. And read the Bible. Then you'll understand."

"I understand enough." Her mother gripped the banister tightly. While Dorry searched for a good answer, a holy answer, one God would give, her mother turned to go back upstairs. "Well, it's past my bedtime. At least tell your friend it's rude to call after ten o'clock at night."

"I will, Mom," Dorry said. But she was angry and upset again. She'd lost the peace Angela had given her.

CHAPTER SEVENTEEN

"OKAY, TELL ME EVERYTHING," Marissa breathed.

She and Dorry were both lying on their stomachs across Marissa's bed, their usual pose for sharing secrets and gossip. The familiar room around them felt as much like home as Dorry's own—more so now that Dorry's belongings were all transplanted to Indianapolis. Dorry's initials were right beside Marissa's on the back of Marissa's dresser. Dorry's face smiled (or grimaced) out from half the photos stuck into the sides of the mirror. But there were changes in the room that Dorry had noticed right away: Unfamiliar books were stacked on the desk. An unfamiliar corsage was wilting on the cluttered bulletin board—not from a dance, Marissa had reluctantly admitted, but from marching band recognition night. A pile of unfamiliar fabric lay in the corner from some new craft project of Marissa's.

"You want to know everything?" Dorry hedged.

"Well, you know nothing around here ever changes. So you're the one with all the news. Except, oh, did I tell you about Steve VaugŸ and Ashley Hanover?"

"No, what?"

"They broke up."

"They were dating?"

"All fall. Hot *and* heavy."

"Oh," Dorry said. She was curious—it was hard to imagine tall, lanky Steve with short, fat Ashley. But gossip didn't seem the right opening to converting Marissa. She rubbed a worn spot on Marissa's bedspread. "Did I tell you about Fishers?"

"Who's that? Don't tell me—you're dating someone." In her excitement, Marissa rolled over and perched cross-legged on the bed. "I told you that new haircut would work wonders."

Dorry felt a slight pang, remembering her crush on Brad. What if things were different, and she were sitting here telling Marissa about dating Brad? Marissa would love that. But her crush on Brad had been lust. It was wrong. Evil. She pursed her lips. "Fishers isn't a who, it's a what," Dorry said. "This has nothing to do with hair."

She could hear the irritation in her own voice. If God wanted Marissa saved so badly, why didn't He send down a bolt of lightning and do it Himself? Dorry thought of the kind of answer Angela would give to that question. And Marissa was her best friend. How could she let her go to hell? Guiltily, she sat up and tried again.

"Fishers is, well, it's kind of like a church, but it's not boring and useless. It's real. It's—they have all the answers about God and Jesus and how people have to live to keep from going to hell. You have to believe in Jesus and be baptized as a Fisher."

Marissa giggled. "Geez, Dorry, you sound like a Holy Roller."

"No, the Holy Rollers are fanatics. This is the truth. This is the only church that's right. Wouldn't—" Dorry cleared her throat. "Wouldn't you like to join?"

Marissa looked puzzled. "Dorry—you really believe this stuff?"

Dorry nodded. She watched Marissa's face. Marissa looked uncertain at first, then guarded, as if she'd put up a screen to keep Dorry from seeing what she was really thinking. Dorry felt as insulted as if Marissa had physically pushed her away.

"You know everyone in my family goes to the Methodist Church," Marissa finally said. "If they go anywhere. Let's talk about something else. What are kids wearing in Indianapolis?"

"That's not nearly as important as Fishers," Dorry said. "That's just—frivolous. I wanted to tell you about something that really matters."

"You did tell me. Now I'm asking about something else."

"But don't you worry about your eternal soul?"

"No," Marissa said. "I mean, it's not like I don't believe in Jesus and God and all that." She lowered her voice as if it were slightly embarrassing to be caught talking about religion.

"But—"

"Come on, Dorry, lighten up. Listen, don't you want to know why Steve and Ashley broke up? Nobody's supposed to know, but Ashley told Shawn, who told Nikki, who told me—"

Distantly, Dorry listened to Marissa's account of the doomed relationship. Marissa started with the first date, so when she finally ended with, "—Can you believe that?" Dorry discovered she'd missed the main part of the story. She suddenly didn't care either. All she could think about was having to call Angela that night and admitting that she'd failed to convert Marissa.

"Marissa, I know you're Methodist and all, but couldn't you try giving Fishers a chance? We could just pray together, and then—" Dorry realized nobody had told her what to do once she converted someone. Everybody had to be baptized, but surely she couldn't do that by herself. And Marissa wouldn't have anyone to be her discipler, as a Fisher all alone in Bryden. If Angela had really expected her to succeed, wouldn't she have told her what to do?

Marissa was scooting back on the bed. "Geez, Dorry, why are you acting so weird?"

"I'm not acting weird."

They looked at each other. Finally Dorry sighed and said, "Anybody else break up lately?"

She left less than an hour later. She had intended to spend the whole day with Marissa, but she suddenly couldn't stand the gossip she used to love. Wasn't gossiping like judging others? Wouldn't God disapprove? And Marissa kept giving her strange looks, as if she didn't recognize her.

Walking the four blocks home in the cold, Dorry could easily imagine Marissa telling everyone about her at school on Monday. Lots of people would ask, "Hey, how's Dorry? Wasn't she back for Thanksgiving?" And Marissa would answer, "Oh, she's really weird now. She's some sort of religious nut."

Probably Dorry's niece Heidi would be spreading her version of the big scene at Thanksgiving, so by the end of the day Monday everybody at Bryden High would think Dorry had flipped out. It wasn't like she'd ever been

Miss Popularity anyhow, but at least people used to think she was sane. Embarrassment came over her in waves. She stopped and turned around. Maybe she could tell Marissa she was just acting—pretending to get practice for a school play or something. She could stay the rest of the day and act normal, and Marissa would forget her talking about Fishers.

She started walking back toward Marissa's. But turning around was like changing the tape in her head. Instead of picturing everybody talking about her on Monday, she remembered her Bible Study group talking about persecution. Everybody had agreed that God and Fishers were more important than anyone's opinion.

"People are going to make fun of you. And who cares?" Angela had asked in her smooth, confident voice. "We know we're right. God knows we're right. When they're in hell and you're in heaven, you'll have the last laugh."

Dorry shoved her cold, chapped hands in her pockets and turned around again. She hoped nobody'd seen her.

CHAPTER EIGHTEEN

DORRY SAT WITH ELEVEN others in her newly formed E Team. *E* stood for "evangelism," Angela had revealed only the night before, when she told Dorry she had to go to the meeting.

"But—I've got a chemistry test the next day," Dorry said. "I do Fishers stuff five nights a week. Can't I skip this?" She didn't add that her parents acted worried now every time she told them she was doing something with Fishers. And they didn't even know about most of the Fishers events she attended, because they were away so much. Was it a sin to deceive them? Or was it fair defense against the Devil, since they were unbelievers trying to come between her and God? Her mother had gone so far as to get up early Sunday morning to suggest a special mother-daughter shopping trip, to lure her away from the Fishers service.

"No, thank you," Dorry had said guiltily. But shouldn't she feel righteous, choosing God over the possibility of new clothes?

Angela didn't seem to see anything righteous about Dorry. "Oh, Dorry, of course you can't skip the E-Team meeting," she said. "How could you even ask? After you failed so miserably over Thanksgiving—you should be begging me for things to do to get back in God's good graces."

Dorry felt the hot flush of guilt that had become a constant companion since Thanksgiving. If only she'd tried harder . . . maybe if she'd turned around and gone back to Marissa's, not to try to act normal, but to convince Marissa to join Fishers . . . It'd been more than a week since Thanksgiving, and Dorry only wanted Angela to forget the whole thing.

"Can't you forgive me?" Dorry said. "Didn't Jesus forgive?"

"Well, *sure*," Angela said. "When people were sincere. How can I know you're really repentant until you show that you have changed? Have you given up your sinful desire to overeat? Have you made a genuine effort to convert anyone?"

Dorry didn't eat the rest of the day. Then she was too weak to think of speaking to anyone, let alone converting them.

Now Dorry sat on a stranger's bed trying to remember chemical formulas. If she convinced herself she could keep all the positives and negatives straight in her head, she'd only have to study for an hour when she got home. She was concentrating on ions so hard that she almost forgot to bow her head when everyone began to pray. The prayer bounced around the room. Dorry tuned out most of it until she heard Angela's voice.

"—and we pray for our sister, Dorry Stevens, who comes to you humbled and broken, among the fallen. Thank you for granting us the mercy to give her another chance. Please help her to redeem herself and become a useful member of your kingdom," Angela prayed.

Anger boiled in Dorry's stomach. How dare Angela pray like that, in front of people Dorry didn't even know. It made Dorry sound truly evil. That was part of the prayer she'd seen on the Fishers' list for drug addicts and prostitutes. Dorry had only skimmed it because she'd never imagined herself meeting people like that.

Angela's elbow dug into Dorry's ribs. Dorry looked up, startled. "Your turn," Angela whispered, loud enough for everyone to hear.

"I pray—" Dorry began haltingly. She couldn't say any of the words that sprang to mind: That Angela stop acting so superior. That I finally manage to convert someone so Angela will quit lording it over me. That you somehow erase Thanksgiving from everyone's memory. The silence in the room grew. Dorry could hear the people around her breathing. How long would they wait for her to say something? Someone cleared his throat. Dorry rushed to speak. "I pray—we pray for forgiveness. For everyone."

Then she couldn't think of anything else. After another long, uncomfortable pause, someone across the room took up the prayer. After the "Amen," everybody looked up. Were they all staring at her?

Mark, the leader of the group, stood up. It was his bedroom they were crowded into. He was older—a college student, Dorry thought. He lived in his own apartment, but it was an apartment so small the bed doubled as a couch and the kitchen was in the same room.

"Evangelism is the most important job of Fishers," he said. "People out there are in darkness, in evil, and only we have the light to bring them to goodness. Look around."

Self-consciously, Dorry did. Most of the others were probably high school students. She could tell that everyone was sitting in discipling pairs—she thought she could pick out the person being discipled in each case. They sat with shoulders slumped, eyes downcast. Only the disciplers attempted to look straight at her, and then it was Dorry who looked away. After Angela's prayer, she felt as guilty as if she really were a drug addict or a prostitute.

The strange thing about the E Team was that, for the first time since the retreat, Dorry was in a small group that included males. She wasn't the only one who noticed, either, because one guy, the least-humble looking of the disciplees, whistled. "Hey, look! Girls!"

Mark laughed, but it was a restrained laugh that held back any real amusement. "Yes. We trust that you are all mature enough in your faith now not to be distracted by members of the opposite sex. We've discovered that, for some reason, evangelism is done best by males and females together. If you'll think back, a mixed pair probably converted you."

Brad and Angela, Dorry thought. Since the retreat, she'd barely seen Brad, except briefly at Fishers parties or at the big Sunday services. He was always polite, but in a hurry. Just thinking about him now made her feel embarrassed and ashamed. How could she have told Angela that she lusted after him?

"To be effective evangelists, you must know and trust each other intimately," Mark continued. "I want you to turn to another person—not your discipler—and confess your worst sin."

People twisted and turned, jockeying for position. There was scattered nervous laughter. Angela half shoved Dorry toward a boy with glasses sitting on the floor.

"I'm Zachary," he said.

171

Dorry looked closer. "Oh. From the retreat," she said. "I'm Dorry. Remember?"

She hadn't recognized him before because he looked so different—no longer merely thoughtful, but anguished, practically tortured. He had the same wild look in his eye that crazy people on street corners wore. It hurt to look at him. Dorry remembered confessing to Angela in her first discipling session that she'd felt attracted to Zachary, as well as Brad. The thought made her blush with shame all over again—both that she'd felt lust, if that's what it was, and that she'd felt it for this guy. He was much too disturbed looking to think of romantically.

He didn't notice Dorry's blush. He seemed only barely aware of her presence. "Yes. The retreat. You're Chocolate."

Dorry grimaced, the nickname now just another spur to guilt. She was so hungry, just the mention of food made her mouth water. But that was sin, Angela said, sin to want to eat all the time, putting her body's longing for food ahead of her soul's longing for God.

Zachary didn't see Dorry's grimace. He was looking down, as if unable to face her while he confessed. "My sin is—I have doubts, terrible doubts," he murmured shamefully. "What if Fishers aren't right? What if it's Buddhists who have all the answers? Or Taoists?"

Dorry had never heard of Taoists. "I don't know,"

she said. "Pastor Jim and the others seem pretty sure of themselves."

"But shouldn't everybody who believes in a particular religion be absolutely sure that they're right?" Zachary asked. "Aren't Buddhists or Muslims just as sure?"

"I don't know," Dorry said doubtfully. And yet, she did know what she believed. When she was praying—not just mouthing words but truly calling out for God—she often had the sense that He was there, that He cared about her. What she struggled with was everything else in Fishers, the pressure to eat and act and think exactly as Angela commanded. Yet she had found God through Fishers. Surely Fishers was right. She just had to learn to obey.

She was just starting to explain her sin when Mark interrupted. "Okay, now," he said. "How many of you confessed doubts about the Word of God?"

Zachary and three or four others raised their hands.

"Doubts are the work of the Devil," Mark said. "You must stifle all doubts to be an effective evangelist. We're going to do an exercise to end your evil doubtings."

He directed them to sit in a circle on the floor, each one facing the next person's back. Then they put their hands on each other's shoulders. Dorry could feel Zachary's thin, bony shoulder blades through his shirt. She couldn't see the boy who touched her.

Mark turned out the light. "Now, massage," Mark commanded. "And repeat, 'I am the way and the truth and the life; no one comes to the Father, but by me.'"

They sat for nearly an hour like that, in the dark, chanting and rubbing each other's backs. Dorry felt the words were engraved in her mind, on her back, on every inch of her skin. When Mark finally said, "Okay, stop," her brain barely recognized words that weren't, "I am the way and the truth and the life; no one comes to the Father, but by me."

"That passage is key to evangelism," Mark said. He spoke so softly Dorry had to lean in to hear him over the sound of her own breathing. "You must repeat it for an hour every day, for the next week. Then you'll be ready for your first evangelism trip."

"What are we doing?" someone had the nerve to ask.

"We'll discuss that next week," Mark said, his voice receding as though he were walking away.

He flipped the switch on the wall and everyone blinked rapidly, blinded by the sudden light.

Dazedly, Dorry stood up along with everyone else. She was suddenly bone weary, tired beyond words. How could one hour of sitting in the dark exhaust her so completely?

Everyone was subdued, gathering up coats and murmuring good-byes. Dorry heard a couple of people slip into "I am the way . . ." almost unconsciously, as if barely aware of what they were saying. Angela actually had to take Dorry's hand to lead her out of Mark's apartment.

When Dorry got home, she fell asleep immediately, her chemistry book left unopened on the desk.

CHAPTER NINETEEN

DORRY GOT A D on her chemistry test. In a panic, she hunted Angela down after the tests were handed back. The halls were crowded and Dorry bumped into several people. Angela was at her locker, leisurely combing her hair.

"I can't do so much Fishers stuff," Dorry said. "Look."

Dorry held the red-marked test up to Angela's face. Angela's blue eyes flickered briefly toward the paper. "I have to do better than this," Dorry said. "My parents will kill me if they find out. Remember . . . remember what I told you about wanting to go to college?"

Dorry's voice was squeaky and panicky. She'd been up until two the night before, praying and doing homework after Bible Study. Then she'd gotten up at five thirty to get in her hour of morning prayers before school. She'd practically fallen asleep in history class, and even now, jolted awake by the chemistry results, she felt too tired to think straight. She could feel the beginning of tears threatening at the back of her throat.

Angela took hold of Dorry's shoulders. "Dorry, calm down. Remember your priorities. So what if you got a D? 'Do not lay up for yourselves treasures on earth, where moth and rust consume and where thieves break in and steal, but lay up for yourselves treasures in heaven, where neither moth nor rust consumes and where thieves do not break in and steal.' Matthew 6:19 and 20. Focus on your heavenly grades, not something that's just going to pass away. 'For where your treasure is, there will your heart be also.' Matthew 6:21."

In her exhaustion, Dorry had to look at her chemistry test to be sure it wasn't already crumbling and turning to dust. It wasn't. The big red *D* was fresh and crisply formed. "You used to be proud that I got good grades," she whimpered.

"That was before you were a Fisher," Angela said. "It showed you could work hard. Now you have more important work to do. God's work."

Dorry began to cry, right there in the hall. Other kids sidestepped her, some pointedly not looking at her, others staring. Dorry heard someone whisper, "—one of those Fishers—" Dorry worried about the witness she was giving. Being mocked for God's sake was holy. But she was only crying for herself.

Angela sighed and took a Kleenex from a small pack in her locker. She gently wiped Dorry's eyes and helped her blow her nose. It made Dorry feel about five years old. Dorry liked that.

"There, there," Angela said. "Cry. It's okay."

The halls began clearing out around them. The bell was going to ring soon. Angela put her arm around Dorry's shoulder and guided her back toward her chemistry class, for lab.

"Think about 1 Corinthians 13:11. Paul wrote, 'When I was a child, I spoke like a child, I thought like a child, I reasoned like a child; when I became a man, I gave up childish ways.'" Angela said. "You must do that, too. Before you were a Fisher, you needed people to make you feel good about yourself, to praise you. You'll learn how to do that for others in the E Team. Then when you were a new Fisher, you had to be treated as gently as a baby. But now you're Level Two. You need to stop thinking about yourself." Angela gave her a little shove, and Dorry ended up inside the classroom door just as the bell rang.

"To your lab station, Miss Stevens," the teacher said. "Pronto." The look he gave her was not mean, but somehow that made her want to cry harder. What if she explained to him why she'd done so poorly on the test? What if she told him—or *someone*, anyway—about Fishers? She didn't want to describe the good "You should be converted" version of it. She wanted to tell somebody the way she felt now: I hate it. It's ruining my life. I don't even feel like me anymore.

Dorry was surprised by the force of the bitter words running through her head. How could she think like that when Fishers had saved her from loneliness, from sin, from hell? She didn't know. She couldn't think. Which thoughts were hers, and which were the Devils?

Dorry stood at her lab station utterly lost. She let her lab partner do all her work for her.

CHAPTER TWENTY

THERE WAS ANOTHER FISHERS party that Saturday night.

This time, since Dorry wasn't an outsider or a new Fisher, she wasn't supposed to enjoy it, Angela told her sternly at her Thursday discipling session. She had work to do.

"I can take care of the snacks," Dorry said eagerly, trying to show she was going to be a good sport about it. Having just confessed her anger in chemistry, she knew she needed lots of virtuous acts to make up for her sins. "And I won't eat any of them. Honest."

Angela shook her head. "Sorry, Chocolate."

The nickname brought the familiar, bitter taste of guilt into Dorry's mouth. Dorry winced, as if Angela had hit her.

"Really. Food doesn't matter to me now—"

"This isn't about that," Angela said. "You can't help with snacks because you have an E-Team assignment." Angela filled her in on the details: Dorry was supposed to help evangelize a girl named Kayla Spires, a freshman at Crestwood. Kayla was very insecure and shallow and needed to be led gently.

"Over there," Angela said, as they stepped into the now-familiar apartment-complex clubhouse.

Dorry followed Angela toward a petite, blond-haired girl. There wasn't time to admire the balloons and Christmas decorations, or to listen to the soft music enveloping them. Angela stopped a few paces back and whispered in Dorry's ear: "Remember your instructions?"

Dorry nodded and began reciting. "Smile. Be friendly. Show how happy I am to be a Fisher." Dorry gulped, a rebel voice in her head asking, *What if I'm not happy?* Was she the only Fisher who wasn't? What was wrong with her?

"And?" Angela prompted.

"Above all, focus on Kayla, not myself."

"Good." Angela nodded approvingly. "You'll do fine."

Dorry stumbled forward.

"Kayla?" Angela was saying with a warm smile. "I'm really glad to see you here tonight. I'm Angela and this is Dorry."

"Hi," Dorry said.

Kayla turned to them with a jerk of her head. She reminded Dorry of a hummingbird, all nervous energy and fluttery motion. "Hi," Kayla said. "Are you guys new, too? I didn't know—I hate parties where I don't know people, but Lisa said everybody was nice."

Dorry recognized the other girl standing with Kayla from several Fishers functions. Kayla's future discipler, Dorry thought. There was a guy there, too—Brad. He only glanced at Dorry and Angela, giving them the barest of nods.

"We already performed our human sacrifice for the night, so you're safe," he said in his familiar joking voice.

"Brad!" Lisa said. "What if she believes you?"

Kayla giggled. "I don't. I can take a joke from a cute boy." She smiled at him, and Brad smiled back fondly. Dorry remembered that smile.

"So you're a freshman?" Dorry said awkwardly. She glanced at Angela, hoping she'd asked a good question.

Kayla nodded. "I was terrified of starting high school, and then my dad got transferred over the summer, so I really had to start over. But I've made some good friends already. There are lots of nice people here."

"I just moved here, too—" Dorry started to say, but was silenced by a look from Angela. "You've already made friends?"

"Oh, sure. It's not that hard," Kayla said with a giggle.

Maybe for you, Dorry wanted to say bitterly.

Unbidden, another evil sentence formed in her head: *The only friends I could make were just interested in my soul.* She pushed the thought away as if it were the Devil himself trying to set up camp in her mind. Which, of course, it was.

"Between your charming personality, your vivacious wit, and your vast beauty, naturally people are flocking to meet you," Brad was saying. "Just look at us right now." He waved his arm to indicate the circle around Kayla: himself, Lisa, Angela, and Dorry. "If you weren't here, I might have to talk to one of them," he added jokingly. He gestured toward the other girls. Dorry told herself he didn't mean to point directly at her.

"You're such a flirt," Kayla said, with a flirty little laugh of her own. She all but batted her eyes at Brad.

Dorry felt a stab of jealousy. She could never have given Brad a look like that without appearing totally ridiculous. He was probably sincerely interested in Kayla. And she had to face facts: He'd only been pretending with her.

No, no, she told herself. *Focus on Kayla. Devil, begone!*

"Would you like something to eat?" she asked Kayla.

Kayla turned with a jerk, as if she'd forgotten Dorry. "Oh, no, thanks," she said. "Party food is just so fattening, you know?"

Dorry started to say something about her own struggles with food—how she'd love a plate of chips and dip right now! But at the last minute, she remembered she didn't matter, only Kayla did.

"But you're so thin," she said, trying to sound more admiring than jealous. "Why do you worry?"

"So I stay this way," she said. "My dad says butterflies eat more than I do."

Brad laughed. "So you live on air?"

"Could be," Kayla said with a giggle.

Dorry wanted to puke. She wanted to talk to anybody else but this bratty, self-centered, skinny freshman. She looked around. All around the room were similar clusters of four or five people, just like there'd been at every Fishers event she'd gone to. She knew now that they were all set up, designed by whoever planned everything—was it Pastor Jim? Above the music, she could hear people laughing. It all sounded forced. Had she really been fooled before?

"Angela?" she asked. "Can I talk to you? Privately?" Everybody's heads jerked toward her. Angela glared, then instantly smoothed her face into a smile when Kayla looked her way.

"Dorry, you don't really need to do that right now, do you?" Angela gave Dorry a little kick, a reminder that private talks would hardly help save Kayla's soul.

"Yes," Dorry said stubbornly. "I do."

Angela gave a shrug. "No offense, everyone, but—"

"Go ahead," Lisa said.

Kayla looked puzzled. Brad distracted her by slipping his hands over her eyes and joking, "Hey, if they don't want to see us, we don't want to see them, either."

Angela and Dorry went around the corner from the bathroom, to the place where Dorry had heard Angela arguing with Lara at Dorry's first party.

"This had better be good," Angela fumed as soon as they were hidden. "Because, otherwise, you really screwed up. Your next sin number is going to be through the ceiling."

Dorry felt trapped in the tiny alcove. She steeled herself to meet Angela's anger, for once not sorting out which of her thoughts were from the Devil and which were acceptable.

"This is all fake," she said. "Why should I pretend to like Kayla when I really hate her? We know the truth. Why don't we just tell her about Jesus and God and needing to be saved?"

Angela exploded. "That's all you wanted to say?"

Looking down, Dorry nodded.

"Don't you remember what you were like when we first met you?" Angela asked. "Every time we mentioned

God or Jesus, you'd stiffen up, like you were afraid we were a cult and we were going to send you to the airport in a robe to sell flowers. The Devil makes it hard to convert people. It's work. It's like—you have to butter people up before they're ready to be cooked."

"You mean caught," Dorry said. "Fishers catch people." She hardly knew what she was saying. She was tired. She was hungry because she'd practically stopped eating so Angela would believe she didn't love food more than God.

"Whatever," Angela said. She took Dorry's arm. "Just remember. You're not in charge here. When you're evangelizing, you listen to me and the lead evangelizer—in this case, Lisa. And you obey. Got it?"

Frightened, Dorry nodded.

"Good." Angela let go of Dorry's arm, practically pushing her away. "Now get back to work."

Dorry was nice to Kayla the rest of the evening.

At ten, Kayla and the other non-Fishers left and everyone lined up to greet a vanload of new Fishers coming for baptism. Dorry moved in a daze, smiling and hugging each new person as they moved through the receiving line.

"Welcome," she said, over and over again. She watched as each one was baptized, and she congratulated them on the way out. She hoped she smiled widely enough, looked delighted enough. She was one gear rotating again and again in a whole factory turning out new Fishers.

She didn't think at all.

CHAPTER TWENTY-ONE

IT WAS CHRISTMAS VACATION before Dorry knew it. Between Fishers events and semester exams, she was living on two or three hours of sleep a night. She stopped babysitting for two weeks because the Garringers were in Florida, and though she missed the kids immensely, she didn't gain any spare time. Angela gave her extra discipling sessions instead. She ate nothing but rice cakes for an entire week to atone for messing up her E-Team assignment with Kayla. She did no Christmas shopping. Even though the stores were infinitely better in Indianapolis, she figured she could wait to shop in Bryden. She and her parents were to be there for an entire week. She alternated between dreading the trip and longing for it like she'd longed for nothing before in her life.

"Why don't you stay here with me?" Angela asked at

their last discipling session before Dorry was to leave. They were at a Burger King after school—the same Burger King Dorry had gone to with Lara all those months ago. This time, Dorry bought Angela's food, because, as a Level Two, Dorry was supposed to be serving others. Angela had a chicken salad. Dorry had a cup of water, because she was fasting to make up for falling asleep during her prayers the night before. The smell of French fries was driving her crazy.

"What?" she said.

"Why don't you stay here with me over Christmas?" Angela asked again, as patiently as if Dorry were a particularly stupid child who couldn't be expected to remember a simple question for longer than one minute. "Remember how much temptation you faced last time you went to Ohio. And think how much Fishers work we could get done."

Dorry felt a flicker of hope. How easy. She could stay with Angela. Angela expected her to act like a Fisher. She wouldn't ask rude questions or stare at her like she might break into rabid prayer at any moment. Angela would help her follow her commandments, not dump candied yams on her plate when she was supposed to fast.

But a small part of her—a part she now usually labeled as tainted by the Devil—called out forcefully, *No!* She had to escape from Angela, if only for a week.

She wanted to sleep late and skip praying altogether and eat all her mother's best foods: pancakes floating in pools of maple syrup, Christmas cookies by the dozens, thick slices of the Christmas ham. Of course, she'd never be able to do that. She'd have to call Angela every day. She'd have to face Angela when she got back.

"Mom and Dad wouldn't let me stay here," she said dully. She waited for Angela to quote Matthew 11:35, "I have come to set a man against his father and a daughter against her mother." And yet, reading the Bible on her own, Dorry had also found Ephesians 6:1, "Children, obey your parents . . ." Would Dorry dare to mention that? Of course not. She had to remember: Angela was the one who could tell her which part of the Bible to follow when.

But Angela only shrugged. "If Fishers isn't important to you, I can't make you change," she said. "You'll just have to explain it to God on Judgment Day."

"I didn't say I didn't want to stay," Dorry said. "It's my parents."

Angela shrugged again. Coupled with her most disappointed look, the shrug might as well have spoken: *I've worked hard to save you, but if you don't care enough to do God's will, it's not my fault.*

After a second, Dorry asked timidly. "Are there any . . . Do you have any commandments for me while I'm away?"

Angela took a dainty bite of the salad balanced on

her plastic fork. She chewed and swallowed. "You should know what you need to do. Frankly, Dorry, I'm concerned about your soul. You should be a Level Three by now, and discipling your own new Fisher. But your sin numbers are much too high and your virtuous acts are shockingly rare."

"But I try to be a good Fisher," Dorry said.

"Have you converted a single new person?"

"No."

Angela waved her hand as if to say, *There you have it.*

Dorry couldn't stifle a yawn. Angela didn't comment on that, but her raised eyebrows said everything. "No extra commandments for Christmas," Angela said, and stabbed a piece of chicken in her salad.

Dorry watched Angela eating for a full minute before the words registered. "Nothing about food? I don't have to save anyone?" Dorry squinted, puzzled. "This isn't a test or anything, is it?"

Angela put down her fork. "See, Dorry. There's your problem. All you're concerned about is yourself, whether you're going to pass a test or not, what you get to eat, how you rank. And that, 'I don't have to save anyone?' question. If you really were a good Fisher, you would want to save everyone. You wouldn't wait for me to command you to do things. You should be telling me, 'I'm going to do my best to convert two or three people back in Ohio. I'm going to set up Bible Studies. I'm going to hold prayer groups. I'm going to make a difference. I'm going to turn that place into a community of Fishers.' But no, you just ask, 'I don't have to save anyone?'" Angela's imitation was cruel and uncannily accurate. She leaned forward and peered into Dorry's eyes. "All I can do is pray for you. And you should pray for your own soul, too. Frankly, sometimes I wonder if you're really saved."

Suddenly, Dorry hated Angela. The hatred was like a nuclear reaction inside Dorry's gut. A meltdown. She wanted to take Angela's plastic fork and stab it right in her heart. She wanted to slap her. She wanted to kick her, over and over and over again. Dorry was evil, filled with evil. She wanted to kill Angela. It took every ounce of her self-control to make herself bow her head and mumble meekly, "I'll pray."

But she didn't. She went to Bryden and she slept sixteen hours straight the first night, after sleeping the entire trip. She ignored her family, only vaguely noticing their worried looks and worried questions. She barely spoke more than a word at a time—even "yes," "no," and "unh" seemed to require much too much energy. The second day they were home, the day before Christmas, she was sitting zombielike in front of the TV when she suddenly realized her mother was leaning into her face, her nose practically touching Dorry's, and screaming,

"Answer me—do you want to go Christmas shopping?"

"You don't have to yell," Dorry said, with great effort and what she hoped was great dignity.

"I didn't, the first five times," her mother said.

Dorry went and trudged through K-Mart and bought whatever her mother told her to.

The second night she was home, Christmas Eve, Dorry stood in the bathroom, fingering the ring Angela had given her. It was too loose on her hand, now that she'd begun losing weight. It rubbed back and forth. It felt like it was burning her skin.

I could flush it down the toilet, Dorry thought. *I could tell Angela I lost it.* She took it off. Her hand felt light and free. She held the ring over the toilet. It sparkled. She lowered it closer and closer to the water. She dropped it. It floated slowly down, gleaming against the porcelain. She touched the toilet handle. She could get rid of the ring and drop out of Fishers and go back to being herself. She pictured the shiny ring disappearing in a swirl of flushing water. It would end in sewage and muck, its shine hidden forever.

And she would go to hell for rejecting God.

Shaking, Dorry reached into the cold water and picked up the ring. She slid it on the ring finger of her left hand. She held on to the sink because her legs were quaking too much to support her.

Someone knocked at the door. "Ready to go to the Christmas Eve service?" her mother called.

"I can't," Dorry said.

"But you're so religious now—"

"I'm sick." She opened the door and let her mother see that her skin was clammy, her breathing rough, her hair sweat soaked and plastered to her face.

Dorry hid in her room until the rest of the family was gone. Then she sneaked downstairs and sat in front of the Christmas tree. She stared at it until her eyes lost focus and the lights all blurred into one another. What was wrong with her? What had happened to the joy and peace and love she'd felt as a new Fisher? Everything she thought and did now was evil. Staying home from church was evil. But going would have been evil, too, because it was the wrong church, one full of hypocrites who cared nothing about God.

She wanted to call Angela, to confess, to find out what she was supposed to do. But Angela would be at the all-night Fishers Christmas prayer service down-town. Dorry should be there, too. That was what she was supposed to do.

She went to bed. In the morning, she felt better. It was like she really had been sick, like she'd caught some virus of evil that her body had successfully fought. But now, Christmas morning, she was a new person, one actually capable of being a good Fisher. She opened presents with her parents and exclaimed politely over everything. When the rest of the family arrived, she remembered to thank Aunt Emma for the knitted socks. She sat beside Uncle Ed again for Christmas dinner but didn't even flinch when he asked, "I see that ring is on your wedding finger now. Did you run off and get married?"

"No," Dorry explained calmly. "I just lost enough weight to put it on the right finger. It's a sign of my devotion to my church."

Dorry heard the snickers far down the table, and the kids being loudly hushed. She easily ignored it. She passed the candied yams down the table without taking any.

Her uncle looked over at her plate, which contained a carrot stick, three pieces of celery, and a dollop of mashed potatoes. "I reckon you ain't fasting anymore, but you might as well be," he joked.

"I've broken the bondage of being a slave to my appetite," Dorry said. And it was true: The forkful of mashed potatoes she brought to her mouth seemed utterly tasteless. She put her fork down. She wasn't hungry. She looked with distaste at the way Uncle Ed was shoveling in the mountains of food on his plate.

Uncle Ed started a conversation across the table about the price of a new bathroom sink he'd installed the day before.

"Dorry?" her mother called. "Can you help me with something in the kitchen?" Obediently, Dorry followed her mother out. Her mother busied herself sliding more rolls onto a platter that was already full. "This church stuff has gone too far. Can't you just act normal for Christmas?" she asked through clenched teeth.

"I am normal," Dorry said. "I'm better than normal. If you weren't in sin, you would see that."

Dorry's mother whirled around, with amazing speed for someone her age. "That's exactly the kind of thing I mean," she said. "How dare you say that to me."

Dorry saw the tears at the corners of her mother's eyes, but the words playing in her head were about the virtues of being persecuted, not the value of compassion. "I'm only speaking the truth," Dorry said calmly. "Sinners usually don't like truth." She suddenly understood Angela's self-confidence, her air of assurance. It truly didn't matter who was against her. She knew God was on her side.

Dorry's mother practically threw the empty roll pan into the sink. It clattered loudly. "This is a stage you're going through," she hissed. "Your father and I will put up with it if we have to. But you don't have to insult your uncle like that. Or anyone else. I won't allow it."

"Mom?" Denise pushed her way into the kitchen. "Come on back." Denise flashed a dirty look at Dorry, as if she knew Dorry had made their mother cry. Dorry felt a spasm of guilt for upsetting her family. She wondered if she was supposed to follow Denise and her mother out of the kitchen, if they even wanted her back at the table. But she prayed ten times, "Lord, thy will be done. Lord, thy will be done," and her cold calm returned.

CHAPTER TWENTY-TWO

SOMEHOW DORRY NEVER GOT around to seeing Marissa or any other friends over Christmas break. She lived like a hermit in her room, reading the Bible and praying for hours on end. She called Angela twice a day. She barely ate. Once she heard her parents arguing in the hall— "We don't have to put up with this," her father growled. "How do we know she's not in there smoking pot or something?"

"We'd smell it," her mother answered.

Dorry stopped listening. Distantly, she was a little amused that her mother might know what pot smelled like. But she mainly blocked out everything about her parents. She refused every effort they made to draw her out of her room, away from her Bible and prayers. They

198

had rejected God. She could not concern herself with them. She was not allowed to think about anything but Fishers.

Most of the time, she succeeded. By the time they got back to Indianapolis, she could keep herself pure and above sin about two days out of every three. She hoped Angela would notice a big difference in her, a glow that didn't show over the phone. At their first discipling session, just an hour after Dorry was back in town, she had to search for sins to describe.

"I picked my nose once," she finally said, almost defiantly. *Let Angela condemn me for that, if she has to,* she thought. *There's nothing else. And I'm so pure now, so beyond my old selfish self, I don't care if she tells everyone else in Fishers what I did.*

Angela's pen didn't move. "That's not really a sin," she said evenly, not hearing—or ignoring—the challenge in Dorry's voice. "Unless, of course, you did it in front of other people, and that made them question the rightness of being a Fisher. Did you?"

"No."

"Anything else?" Angela's pen hovered over the paper, waiting.

"No."

"Are you sure?"

"I said no. Don't you believe me?"

"Of course," Angela said calmly. "Let's move on. Virtuous acts?"

"Um—" Dorry said.

"You don't have any, do you?" Angela said.

"I was busy praying," Dorry said. "And reading the Bible. I told you. I didn't sin."

Angela's gaze was steady. "It's true your sin numbers are down. They were low for your whole vacation. You know that's good."

Dorry felt a little thrill of victory. See—Angela was proud of her. But Angela was still talking.

"But your virtuous-acts numbers are down, too. You're just a zero all around. You're supposed to be a Fisher, not a zero."

The words cut into Dorry's iron restraint, unleashing a flood of insecurity. *I knew it. Angela always thought I was a zero. And she's right, I am.* And then Dorry was just mad, mad at Angela, mad at herself. Frantically, she tamped down the anger. *God, let me turn from this evil. God, let me turn from this evil.* Biting her cheek, Dorry muttered, "I'm sorry. I'll do better."

After that, every day was a struggle. If she focused on God and obeyed Angela and just didn't think, she was all right. But at the oddest moments, her anger flashed out or she developed evil doubts or questions about Angela's commandments.

When Angela told her she needed to spy on a new member, to make sure he wasn't sneaking cigarettes, Dorry stood outside in the cold for three hours one day, watching a single lighted window. The colder her feet got, the holier she felt. But when she reported back to her E Team, and everyone's eyes focused approvingly on her, a voice whispered in her head, *This is wrong. What you did was evil.*

When her parents got upset that her semester grades came back as mostly Cs with a few scattered Bs, she was serene as they screamed. "No, of course it's not because I'm spending too much time with Fishers," she told them resolutely. "They just expect a lot more at Crestwood. I've got things figured out now. I'll do better." Then she went to her room and sobbed silently, fighting the evil urge to curse Angela, Fishers, and God. "Help me do better. Help me do better," she prayed again and again. She wasn't sure if she was praying for her schoolwork or her soul.

The only place she could relax her guard against evil was at the Garringers', babysitting. She gave piggyback rides to Jasmine and Zoe, played peekaboo with Seth, held their hands in endless games of ring-around-the-rosy and London Bridge. She savored the kids' hugs, which were totally spontaneous and had nothing to do with Dorry's sin numbers or virtuous-acts score. She didn't have to consult Angela before telling Zoe not to stand on the kitchen table. She still felt uncomfortable around Mrs. Garringer, but Mrs. Garringer was only there at the beginning and the end, to say in her melodramatic way, "Dorry, if you only knew what you've done for my sanity!"

Sometimes Dorry felt guilty that she enjoyed Jasmine, Zoe, and Seth so much—that her favorite moments had nothing to do with God or Fishers. But then one day in early January, Angela said, "Dorry, you're not giving enough to Fishers. Saving souls is very expensive. Remember how Jesus asked his disciples to give all that they had?" She waited, as if expecting Dorry to figure out what she needed to do on her own. She didn't. Angela sighed, and added, "You need to give your babysitting money to Fishers."

"All of it?" Dorry asked, feeling the familiar spur of anger and doubt. "But that's my college money."

"If God wants you to go to college, He'll provide a way."

"Okay," Dorry said, though inside she was seething. With Angela watching, she signed over a big check, clearing out her bank account. She hated herself for it. She hated herself for hating herself. She hated God and Angela both. She signed her name carefully.

And then, handing the check over, she felt suddenly free. *Look what I can do. Look what a wonderful Fisher I am.*

After that, when she began enjoying the kids too much, she simply told herself her work was holy, because she was babysitting to earn money for Fishers.

Sometimes she even believed it.

CHAPTER TWENTY-THREE

PASTOR JIM CAME TO speak to Dorry's E Team. It was a momentous occasion—some of the girls baked cookies, and Mark, the leader, had clearly put unusual effort into cleaning his apartment ahead of time.

Pastor Jim came into the room like visiting royalty. But his mournful expression instantly changed the festive mood in the room.

"We are failing," he proclaimed sadly.

He sat on the floor. Quickly, everyone sitting on the bed or on Mark's rickety folding chairs slid down to join him. Dorry knew why: Those who want to be first, should make themselves last. No Fisher could sit in comfort while Pastor Jim sat on hard, cracked linoleum.

"We have good news to share," Pastor Jim continued.

"But in the last month, we have won only fifteen new souls for the Lord."

It sounded like a lot to Dorry. But she quickly adjusted her expression to one of sorrow, to match everyone else in the room.

"Search your souls," Pastor Jim said. "Can you account for this failure?"

Angela answered first. "We don't try hard enough," she said. "We let our own sinful desires get in the way of evangelism."

Dorry felt a pang of guilt that Kayla, the girl she'd been responsible for at her first Fishers party as a Level Two, had stopped having anything to do with Fishers, and told Lisa, her potential discipler, "No offense, but some of you people are weird."

Pastor Jim was nodding thoughtfully. "God has spoken to me," he said. "When I started Fishers three years ago, He told me to be gentle in our evangelism, to win people over with our love before revealing the glorious news we carry. He said that was the way to sneak past humans' fear of righteousness. But last night, He told me there is no time left for subtlety."

Dorry looked around, to see if anyone else knew what he meant.

"I am sending you forth," he said, "to shopping malls

and street corners, to bus stations and the airport, to every place that people gather, to spread the word directly."

There was silence, then Mark said in a puzzled voice, "No more Fishers parties?"

Pastor Jim shook his head firmly. "Parties are evil," he said.

Dorry was inclined to agree. She hated the ritual of fawning over a new person every week. She no longer infuriated Angela with her questions, but she was still awkward and uncomfortable. Maybe what Pastor Jim wanted—what God wanted—would be easier.

"I am counting on you, the young people of Fishers," Pastor Jim declared. "You are the ones with zeal. You are the ones willing to follow Christ unquestioningly."

Dorry had heard Angela and some of the other disciplers complaining that the older Fishers were just not as committed. And she'd noticed fewer and fewer adults at the Sunday services. Were they dropping out? She'd heard of a few younger Fishers leaving, including Lara, the girl who'd taken her to her first Fishers party. Several of the disciplers had assured Dorry's Bible Study group that they made valiant efforts to win back ones who strayed. But her Bible Study group had all agreed: If the dropouts didn't return, it meant they had never truly been saved. For, knowing the truth, how could anyone choose hell?

"The kingdom of God is relying on you!" Pastor Jim thundered. His voice was overpowering in Mark's tiny apartment. Dorry found it impossible to think at all while he was talking.

She nodded automatically with all the others when they made plans to meet Saturday morning at eight. They would chant "I am the way and the truth and the life . . ." for two hours, then be at the Crestwood Mall when it opened. They'd go in teams of four, and hand out brochures about Fishers and salvation.

But Saturday, as Dorry reached for the door to sneak out to Angela's waiting car, she heard a voice behind her.

"Where do you think you're going?" her father boomed.

"To the mall. With my friends. It's—I left a note."

Her father picked up the scrap of paper from the kitchen table. Dorry had written only, "Be back tonight." Angela had advised her not to tell her parents anything she didn't have to.

"That's it!" her father exploded. "Today of all days—"

Dorry looked at him blankly.

"It's your mother's birthday, for Christ's sake!"

Dorry had forgotten the date. Now she remembered her mother saying something about going out to eat. Were Donny and Denise and their families coming in for the day? Dorry couldn't remember. When her mother had told her the plans, one morning before school, Dorry had been busy praying over breakfast so she could tell Angela she'd gotten her full two hours of prayer in.

"Sorry. I forgot," Dorry said now. "Angela's waiting—" She turned to go, but her father stalked across the room and blocked the door.

"You're not going anywhere, young lady. Not today. You're going to stay home and spend time with your family and be nice to your mother. All day."

"But Angela—" Dorry protested.

"I'm not done," her father said. "You're going to pull your grades back up and get your act together and—"

"My act is together," Dorry said. "I'm doing God's work."

Once she would have felt foolish saying those words to her father. Now she felt holy, sublime. She tried to step around him.

"No!" he shouted. "You're not going anywhere!"

"Let her go," Dorry's mother said quietly behind them.

Dorry and her father both turned.

"Let's not fight this battle today," Dorry's mother said. Her hair was still matted from sleep, and her bathrobe hung unevenly, as though she'd pulled it on in a hurry. She looked old and tired. Her eyes were bleary. "I just want a quiet birthday. If Dorry doesn't want to be here. . ." She stopped and tried again. "If Dorry doesn't want to—" She turned around and went back into her room.

Dorry's father looked at Dorry. He stepped back from the door. "Be back by noon," he growled. "Or else."

"I—" Dorry said.

Outside, Angela honked the horn. Dorry stumbled out the door.

"Did you oversleep?" Angela asked as Dorry slid into the car.

"No," Dorry said dazedly. "My parents—I—I was just talking to my parents."

She knew it was a sin not to tell Angela about the confrontation. Angela needed to know every temptation Dorry faced. Angela could figure out a way for Dorry to avoid having to be back by noon. Probably Angela would even praise her for sacrificing her parents' approval for the good of God's kingdom. But Dorry couldn't listen to praise while her mother's pained, "If Dorry doesn't want to . . ." still echoed in her ears.

Dorry was numb and desperately praying for help by the time they reached the mall. She said, again and again, "Are you saved? You must be born again to avoid the fires of hell." But she didn't listen to people's responses. She didn't care that most people threw the brochures in the nearest trash can. In her mind, she kept seeing her mother's hurt face. One minute she could see everything right—Jesus had said he would come between parents and children. Defying her father was like defying the Devil. Her parents were unbelievers. But the more she prayed, the more she doubted. How could the Devil get into her mind even as she talked to God?

Several times she almost turned to Angela and cried, "I'm in sin. Help me." What a relief it would be to let Angela take over. But Angela was busy. Dorry clutched her brochures like a lifeline, and asked another stranger, "Are you saved?"

For once, the stranger didn't move away immediately. Dorry actually looked at him. He wore an official-looking blue shirt and a badge that said "Security."

"Can't you religious nuts read?" he asked. "There are signs all over this mall saying, 'No solicitation.'"

"I—" Dorry gulped. "We're just evangelizing."

"Do it somewhere else. It's not allowed here."

Dorry felt a rush of hope. Maybe her decision was made for her. She glanced at her watch. Eleven fifteen. She could be home by noon.

"Wait a minute—what are you talking about?" Mark protested, rushing to Dorry's side.

"Soliciting—or evangelizing, if that's what you call it—isn't allowed inside the mall. This is private property, and the store owners don't want your kind scaring away the shoppers."

"It's a free country. We can spread the word of God anywhere we wish," Mark said. His stance was brave: chin held high, scrawny chest thrust forward like a boxer before the match.

"Oh, brother," the security guard said, shaking his head. "Let me put it this way: Stop harassing people or I call the cops."

"We harass no one. We are doing the will of God," Mark said. "Arrest us if you have to. We will be martyrs for God's word." He held his wrists out as if he were waiting for handcuffs.

Dorry thought, *Happy birthday, Mom. Can you get me out of jail?* Her parents would never forgive her. She leaned over and vomited at the base of a potted tree.

CHAPTER TWENTY-FOUR

EVEN AS SHE RETCHED, Dorry knew that throwing up was a reprieve. She was sick. Angela would have to take her home. She wouldn't be arrested. She was sick. She wouldn't have to go out to eat with her parents and endure their wrath about Fishers.

When she got home, Donny and Denise and their families were all milling about the tiny apartment. Dorry mumbled hellos and said, "Happy birthday, Mom," and headed straight for bed.

"Wasn't she sick all Christmas break, too?" Donny's voice rumbled behind her. Dorry put the pillow over her ears so she didn't have to hear.

She stayed home from the Fishers service on Sunday because she was sick, and sat like a zombie in the midst of her boisterous family. She avoided her father. Angela called several times, and gave her lengthy discipling sessions over the phone.

"Pastor Jim thinks the Devil intervened with you vomiting and kept us from our God-given glory of being martyrs for Christ," she reported Sunday night. "You aren't really sick, are you?"

"No," Dorry whispered, though she didn't really know. If in doubt, confess.

Angela made a clicking noise with her tongue. "Oh, Dorry. You are so deep into sin. Are you even saved?"

"Of—of course I am!" Dorry insisted. "You told me I was."

"Maybe the Devil fooled me," Angela said with a bitter laugh.

Dorry's stomach churned. It was empty—she hadn't eaten in two days, even rice cakes. She felt light-headed. She saw her father watching her across the room. She took the phone around the corner.

"Angela," she whispered. "Maybe I'm just not cut out for evangelism. Doesn't it say in the Bible that different people have different talents? That we're the body of Christ and some people are eyes and some people are ears and so on? Maybe God wants me to do something else for his kingdom."

"Do you know what verse that is? Can you quote it exactly?" Angela asked.

"N-no," Dorry mumbled. "I just found it on my own. We haven't done that verse in Bible Study—"

"Exactly," Angela snapped. "And do you know why? That's the kind of thing that can confuse a Level Two Fisher. Listen—you read what I tell you to read, and you do what I tell you to do. And you will evangelize!"

Angela ordered her to reread the Bible Study verses she'd memorized fifty times each to make up for her sin, and to pray for three hours a day for God to reward her evangelism next week at the mall. For they would be going back. Dorry didn't dare ask what would happen if they were arrested.

Shaking, Dorry hung up. She sneaked back to her room and turned out the lights so her parents wouldn't try to talk to her. She could avoid them during the week, because they were both on evening schedules. As for next weekend . . . she tried not to think about the next weekend. All she could think about was evangelism. It was all that mattered.

Every Fishers event she went to that week pounded home that message. "You think your salvation is secure," Pastor Jim roared at the Wednesday night service. "How can you sit there and think like that, when the unsaved are all around you, drowning in their sins, and you refuse to help them? You can pull them into the lifeboat. You can give them a hand. You can throw them a line. The

Holy Spirit has put every lifesaving tool known to man at your fingertips. If you do not use them, you are as guilty as any of the unrepented. I tell you now, and you can remember it in hell—you will burn, too!"

Dorry felt the fire of his words burning into her soul. The crowd around her erupted into screams—cheers, maybe, or shrieks of fear. Dorry couldn't tell. She wanted to go someplace quiet, away from Pastor Jim's driving voice, away from the crowd's pushing roar. She wanted to hide. But there was no time after the service—she was assigned to talk to a girl named Jane. She was supposed to make sure that Jane saw no doubt or dismay—nothing less than perfection—in anything connected to Fishers. Woodenly, Dorry smiled and chatted, and agreed with false cheer—sure, Pastor Jim might have sounded a little harsh, but he had a reason. God was harsh, too. But only toward sinners. He gave his true children only love.

After that, there were extra atonement discipling sessions, extra Bible study, extra prayer. Dorry had no minute to herself. Maybe she didn't want to hide anyway. Maybe it was the Devil telling her that. Maybe what she wanted most was to save someone, anyone, so Angela would quit harping on her failure.

It was Friday afternoon, in the midst of babysitting the Garringer kids, that Dorry saw an answer. She hadn't slept more than two hours a night for the past three nights, and she hadn't eaten all day, so the answer came slowly, squeezed like the last drop of ketchup from an almost-empty bottle: of course. She should convert the Garringer children. The children were young and unsullied except by original sin. They would come easily to the Lord. She should have done it months ago.

"Jasmine, Zoe, come over here," Dorry said weakly. The two girls were jumping onto and off of the couch, while Seth watched and clapped in time to a tape of nursery-rhyme songs.

"Don't want to," Jasmine said, and stuck out her tongue.

Dorry reconsidered the "unsullied" notion. "You must," she said. "Or I'll turn off the music."

"I'll come," Zoe said. She tugged on Jasmine's hair. "You too."

Jasmine screamed as if Zoe had scalped her. "Ow, ow—don't do that! Dorry, make Zoe take a time out!"

"Not now," Dorry said. She pulled both girls down so they were sitting on the couch. She crouched, facing them, her arm across their legs so they couldn't get up. "Behave and listen. Do either of you know who God is?"

"Someone big," Jasmine said.

"Like Daddy?" Zoe asked. She giggled. "Daddy's bigger than anybody."

"Not bigger than God," Jasmine said. "But I think he's just pretend."

"No," Dorry said. "God's real. He's kind of like—everybody's father."

Zoe thought that was funny, and giggled harder.

"Stop laughing. This is serious," Dorry said. She cleared her throat. She wanted to tell the girls about God's love, but that wasn't the way to save people now. The parties and fun were over. People didn't listen unless you talked about hell.

"When you are bad, your mommy and daddy punish you, right?" she said. "That's what God does, too. And we're all bad, some of the time. So the way God punishes people, is, when they die, they go to a very bad place. It's called hell. There's fire there all the time—"

"We're supposed to stay away from the fire," Zoe said confidently, pointing to the family-room fireplace.

"You can't stay away from it in hell. It's everywhere. And everybody there gets burned up, all the time."

Zoe and Jasmine were quiet now, their eyes big and scared. "But they don't die?" Jasmine asked.

"They're already dead. They can't die more. So they just keep burning and burning forever."

"Does it hurt?" Zoe asked.

"Yes. A lot. More than anything in your whole life. It hurts all the time. And people scream and scream, from the pain, but it never stops," Dorry said. "It's awful and it never stops and no one can make it stop, not even your mommy and daddy."

Zoe started to cry. "I don't want to go there. You can't make me!"

"No, no, just listen. I can't make you, but God can. And he will, unless you do what he says."

"I don't like God," Jasmine said. "He made my sister cry."

Zoe pushed away Dorry's arm on her lap. "You're bad," she said. "I don't like you anymore."

"Zoe, just listen. It's okay," Dorry said. Somehow, she hadn't pictured this. "You don't have to go to hell. You can accept Jesus and be saved, and then you can save your mommy and daddy and Seth and all your friends, so they won't burn either. You don't want everybody you know to burn up, do you?"

"No! No! Don't make me burn up!" Zoe shrieked. "Stop it! Stop it! Mom-mee!"

She careened out of the room, sobbing. Dorry chased her, calling, "Zoe, wait!"

Zoe pounded on the door of the back room Mrs. Garringer used for a studio. "Mommy, Mommy, Dorry says you and Daddy and Jasmine and Seth and me are going to burn up in hell. I don't want to burn up! I don't want you to burn up—"

The door opened.

"I'm sorry, Mrs. Garringer, I'll get her calmed down—" Dorry said. "Zoe, what I said was—"

Mrs. Garringer flashed Dorry a look of sheer fury as she bent to hug Zoe. Zoe sobbed into her mother's neck. "Mommy, God is going to burn us up. Don't let him! I hate him!" Zoe was in hysterics.

Jasmine came running into the room and grabbed her mother's knees, crying to be picked up, too. Seth crawled after his sister, wailing, "Ma-ma! Ma-ma!"

"Seth, here, you're okay." Dorry tried to pick him up, but he screamed and tried to wiggle out of her grasp, reaching for his mother. Helplessly, Dorry let him slide to the ground. He tugged on Mrs. Garringer's legs, trying to stand up. Jasmine pushed him down, trying to keep her mother to herself. He screamed louder. She screamed louder.

"I'm sorry, Mrs. Garringer," Dorry said. "I didn't mean to scare them. I only wanted to tell them about God—"

She had to shout to make herself heard over everyone crying and Zoe screaming, over and over again, "I don't want to burn up!"

"Get out of my house," Mrs. Garringer said fiercely. She crouched and hugged all of her children to her. They burrowed into her clothes, their faces hidden. Their cries were muffled. Mrs. Garringer soothed them—"Shh, shh, it's all right. Nobody's going to hurt you." Then she glared up at Dorry. "I said get out. Now."

"But—" Dorry couldn't believe she'd heard Mrs. Garringer right. How could this be happening? If only she could explain, make Mrs. Garringer understand. But what she heard herself say was, numbly, "My ride's not here."

"I don't care," Mrs. Garringer said. She hugged her children closer.

"But—it's cold out."

Mrs. Garringer yanked her purse down from the counter by one purse strap. With one hand, she pulled out her billfold and, without looking at them, grabbed some bills out of the center. She flung the money at Dorry. Zoe screamed louder the whole time Mrs. Garringer's arm was away from Zoe's shoulders.

"Walk down to the store on the corner and call a cab," Mrs. Garringer said. "Just leave."

For a minute, Dorry couldn't move, not even to catch the dollar bills floating toward the stained kitchen linoleum. A twenty landed on a crushed Cheerio. "Am I—am I fired?" Dorry asked.

Mrs. Garringer said nothing. She patted Zoe's back, smoothed Jasmine's hair, kissed the top of Seth's head.

"I'm fired," Dorry said. "You just fired me." Slowly she turned and walked out of the kitchen. The air she had to move through seemed as thick as concrete. Finally she reached the coatrack in the hall. She pulled on her coat without zipping it and pushed open the front door. The cold air felt like a slap.

She could still hear the children's cries echoing in her ears long after she climbed down the front steps.

CHAPTER TWENTY-FIVE

DORRY WAS SOBBING UNCONTROLLABLY by the time she reached the corner store. She could barely see to put her money in the phone, to dial Angela's number.

"I've done something awful," she wailed into the receiver. "I have to confess. I'll have to atone for the rest of my life."

The kid behind the counter gawked at her, as though she were an alien who'd suddenly materialized between the bread shelves and the bulletin board advertising dog walkers and snow shovelers. Dorry didn't care.

"You've got to help me," Dorry sobbed.

"Calm down," Angela said coldly. She sounded annoyed. "Whatever it is can't be that bad."

"It is," Dorry cried. "It is. I told the Garringer kids

about hell and they cried and cried. They didn't understand. I've destroyed them. It's all my fault."

"You were evangelizing. Right?" Angela asked.

"Yes, but I did it wrong. I shouldn't have—it was all wrong. I shouldn't have said anything to them—"

"Dorry, quit that. I'll be there in a few minutes."

When Angela pulled up in front of the store in her sports car, the kid behind the counter called out, "Hey, hysterical girl, can't you introduce me to your friend?"

Dorry ignored him and ran out to Angela's car. She grabbed the door handle before the car came to a complete stop. She climbed in and tried to bury her face in Angela's shoulder the way Zoe had cried against Mrs. Garringer's. Angela pushed Dorry away.

"Get a grip," she said. She held Dorry steady, by her shoulders, until Dorry slumped back in the passenger seat. "Now, tell me what happened."

Dorry told it all, lingering her description on the sight of Jasmine's and Zoe's horrified faces, on their terrified hysterics, on Mrs. Garringer's anger. When she finished, Angela shrugged.

"So what's the problem?" Angela said. "People turn from the word of God all the time. They are in sin. The Garringers' house is of the Devil, and it is better that you be away from it."

"No, no, I was wrong—I shouldn't have told the girls about hell—" Why couldn't Dorry make Angela understand?

"Do you want me to talk to Mrs. Garringer?" Angela asked.

Dorry didn't, but she did. She wanted someone to make everything better, to turn things back. To make the Garringer kids okay again. To make them love her again.

Angela started the car and turned onto the Garringers' street. She stopped in front of their house, but left the car running.

"Stay here," she said.

Dorry was grateful for the command. She watched Angela climb the steps, rap at the door. She saw Mrs. Garringer open the door a crack. Mrs. Garringer was talking and shaking her head. Then she was listening to Angela. Then she shoved the door shut.

Angela walked back to the car wearing a beatific expression.

"What happened?" Dorry begged. She couldn't look at Angela, couldn't stand that calm, self-satisfied, smug face.

"I told her that she and her household are evil for turning from God. I said she is wallowing in sin. I told her that when she and her children are in hell, she will regret turning you away when you offered a chance at salvation." Angela spoke as casually as if she'd only said "Hello."

Dorry gasped. "You didn't."

"I did." Angela pulled away from the curb. She looked at Dorry. "I am a messenger of God and it is my duty to tell the truth. It's your duty, too."

Dorry wondered if this was what it felt like to be shot. She looked down and felt stunned that her body was whole, unbloodied. There should be a huge, gaping hole right through her middle, a fatal wound from Angela's words. She bent her head. "No," Dorry whispered.

"What?" Angela pronounced the word so precisely that the "t" practically echoed.

Dorry winced. *You're wrong*, she wanted to say. *God couldn't want what you did, what I did. We were wrong.* Out of habit, she held the words back, because anything she thought that was different from what Angela thought had to be of the Devil. But the Devil was bad and God was good, and Dorry knew that what she'd done to Jasmine and Zoe was bad. So it didn't make sense. She tried to summon back the sense of tranquility and holiness she'd felt at the Fishers retreat—her sense of God—but all she felt was shame. The image of Jasmine's and Zoe's horrified faces swam before her eyes.

"If God wanted me to do what I did to Jasmine and Zoe," Dorry said weakly, "I don't want God."

Angela gaped at her. "Dorry, that's blasphemy. How can you say that? Pray for forgiveness. Right now. That's just the Devil talking through you—"

"No," Dorry said. "It's me."

"Dorry, as your discipler, I command you. Pray for forgiveness."

"No," Dorry said again. "I don't want you to be my discipler anymore."

"But as a Fisher—"

"I don't want to be a Fisher anymore."

Dorry barely knew what she was saying. She felt feverish and chilled all at once, so foggy-headed she could barely think, and yet absolutely certain she couldn't let Angela win this time. Once the words were out, "I don't want to be a Fisher anymore," she was overcome with relief. Of course she wanted out. Evangelizing at the mall, being fake at parties, fasting at Thanksgiving—she'd hated Fishers. Why hadn't she left before?

Oh. God. Dorry felt a spasm of grief, to be giving up God. She began weeping.

"Dorry, you can't do this," Angela said impatiently. "You're a Fisher. You're saved. How can you give away God's gift of love and salvation—and suffer eternal damnation—just because of some brats? Come on, now. Repent, and then you can atone and—"

Dorry saw Jasmine's and Zoe's faces again, so innocent. So wounded. "They're not brats," she said. "Let me out. I don't have to listen to this." Dorry reached for the door with both hands. She looked down and saw the Fishers ring on her finger. She shook it off. Even wrapped twice with red yarn at the back, it slid off easily and landed silently on the floor of Angela's car.

Angela stopped at a red light and Dorry jerked the door open and jumped out.

"Wait," Angela yelled after her. "How will you get home?"

"I'll take a bus," Dorry yelled without looking back. The winter wind tore the words from her mouth and whipped her hair into her face. She wasn't sure if Angela had heard her. But she heard Angela scream back, "You are damned, Dorry Stevens. You are one of the lost."

And then Dorry heard Angela pull the door shut. Angela drove on with the traffic and Dorry was left standing in the street, shivering, watching the blue car until it disappeared.

She didn't know where she was.

CHAPTER TWENTY-SIX

DORRY STOOD NUMBLY IN the street until someone honked at her. She walked blindly for several blocks, not even bothering to look for a bus stop. She didn't know anything about the Indianapolis bus system. Angela had been driving her around for months. How would she get home? She didn't even know if she was going in the right direction.

If she hadn't walked right into a pay phone outside a Wendy's, she might have gone on like that for hours, in the cold. As it was, she stared stupidly at the phone for a full minute before an idea occurred to her. A phone. She could call her mother. She put her money in and dialed. A computerized voice told her, "The number you have reached cannot be connected as dialed," three times before she realized the problem: She'd been dialing her mother's Bryden work number. Without an area code it was useless. She didn't know her mother's number in Indianapolis.

Dorry stared at the phone a while longer before it occurred to her to go into the Wendy's and ask for a phone book. She scanned the list of nursing homes—was it Pleasant View? Pleasant Years? Happy Years? *I will never be happy again,* she thought. *I've given up God.*

She went back to the phone. "Mommy," she wailed into the receiver, "come get me."

When her mother picked her up forty-five minutes later, still huddled outside the Wendy's, she was praying, "Oh, God, what have I done? What do I do now?" But what right did she have to talk to God?

Her mother was jubilant. "Dorry, I'm so glad you're leaving that church," she said. "Your father and I were trying to think of ways—oh, never mind. You've done the right thing now. We can get back to normal. I talked my supervisor into letting me count this as an extra-long dinner break. Let's go somewhere and celebrate. What do you want? Perkins? Bob Evans? Shoney's?"

Dorry's stomach growled. She was starving. But the thought of a restaurant dinner—burgers surrounded by French fries, platters overflowing with spaghetti—made her want to throw up. Food was still evil for her. But how could it be, if she'd given up God?

Dorry turned her face to the window. "I don't feel like celebrating. Just take me home."

"Okay," her mother said.

Dorry and her mother drove the rest of the way home in silence. The phone was ringing as they opened the door.

"Have you repented?" Angela's voice rushed at Dorry over the phone. "Are you ready to atone? We'll need an extra-long discipling session for this. I didn't see it, but you were making those kids into a false god. What a grave sin. You must pray for forgiveness immediately. What if you'd been killed in a wreck on the way home?"

For a minute, Dorry could almost picture it. A truck smashing into their car, broken glass and blood everywhere, Dorry dead on the street. And then God as a mysterious voice in the darkness, proclaiming, "Here's another Fisher, not one of the greatest, but still—oh, no . . . You just quit? Too bad. You know where you go."

Dorry bit her tongue so hard she tasted blood. She summoned up the image of Jasmine and Zoe, wailing, because of her. "I don't want any more discipling sessions," Dorry said through gritted teeth. "Ever. I meant what I said about quitting." And then she hung up.

There were more calls after that, starting five minutes after Dorry's mother finished her dinner break and went back to work. For the next week, the Fishers had an uncanny way of knowing when her parents weren't around. Dimly, Dorry realized someone was spying on her—after all, it had happened before. She'd done it herself. Just as dimly, she knew she could take the phone off the hook, or tell her parents, or even call the police. But maybe she deserved the calls.

"God is watching you. He knows your sin," the voices said sometimes. Or "The Devil has you now. There is rejoicing in hell." Or, "You are evil."

"Yes," Dorry whispered after that call. She felt evil. But no, it was the Fishers and God who were evil. Wasn't it?

She still prayed. Prayed for strength when the calls were nice, "But Dorry, you're like a sister to me. How can I let my sister go to hell?" Angela asked on Monday. Sobbing, Dorry hung up without answering.

"Oh, Dorry, we had such hopes for you," Pastor Jim all but purred into the phone on Wednesday. "You were such a promising member . . . Return and all will be forgiven—"

"No," Dorry said.

Her greatest temptation came the next night. "Dorry, old pal, what's this I hear about you losing your mind?" said the voice on the phone.

It was Brad.

Dorry felt the familiar rush of longing. Of lust. Automatically, she thought, "I'll have to confess this to Angela."

But she wouldn't—she never had to confess anything to Angela ever again. "I won't be judging you or anything, but what do you say I come over and we talk about this. We could go out for pizza maybe." Brad's voice was slow and relaxed, practically a drawl. It was warm, too—Dorry could melt in that voice.

"Just you and me? Like—like a date?"

The instant she'd said them, Dorry wanted to draw her words back. Her face burned. She was glad Brad couldn't see her.

"A date? I thought you'd never ask." The teasing Brad was back. "But you know, I only date Fishers. Second Corinthians 6:14."

Dorry didn't have to reach for a Bible. The verse came into her mind unbidden: "Do not be mismated with unbelievers. For what partnership have righteousness and iniquity? Or what fellowship has light with darkness?" She knew what she was. Iniquity and darkness.

"But, hey," Brad continued. "You reconsider your insanity, sure, we can call it a date." He chuckled.

It was the chuckle that did it. Dorry watched her knuckles turn white as she gripped the edge of the kitchen counter. "I—don't—want—to—see—you," she said. "Good-bye."

That night Dorry dreamed that she threw herself at Brad and they started making out and just as she was certain he really loved her, he had never been pretending, she looked at him again and it wasn't Brad at all, but the Devil, with horns and a fiery face and eyes like burning coals. "You're a fool," he bellowed. "Nobody would want you but me. And I'm just trying to fill up hell."

Then she dreamed she was in hell, screaming in pain, and Angela looked down from heaven and said, "I told you so."

The next morning, when Dorry had shakily gotten herself off to school, she saw Angela in the hall. Dorry began bracing herself to speak—she would say, "Hi," but nothing else, she decided—when Angela breezed past her, looking right through her. It was like Angela's eyes no longer registered Dorry's image.

It was the same way with Brad later in the day, when Dorry was coming out of study hall. She was right in front of him—he couldn't *not* see her—but somehow he didn't.

At lunch she sat two chairs down from her usual Bible Study group, so close she could read the small print in some of their Bibles. No one glanced her way. And then she knew: For the Fishers, she no longer existed.

"I'm a ghost," she whispered in bed that night, in the dark. "Am I a ghost to you, too?"

She wasn't really sure who she was talking to.

CHAPTER TWENTY-SEVEN

DORRY WAS EATING ALONE. Again.

It didn't matter now. She didn't care who saw her. The
school cafeteria buzzed around her, with kids laughing,
joking, yelling. She was on another planet. She chewed
her food doggedly, not even tasting the special treat her
mother had taken to slipping into her bag, declaring,
"You're losing weight too fast, honey. You're starting to
look peaked. This'll perk you up." Today it was a generous slice of brownie fudge pie. Dorry put it down after
one bite and forgot to pick it up again.

It'd been two weeks since she'd left Fishers. Her parents wanted to send her back to Bryden. "You've got to
get over this church thing," her mother fretted. "If you
just go home—"

Dorry pictured herself walking down the hall with

her old friends back at Bryden High School.

"Dorry, you're so thin now," Marissa would rave. "Let's do your hair a little differently, and you'll have all the guys asking you out."

Would Dorry dare answer truthfully? *I don't care about hair. I don't care about guys. I'm in hell. I have condemned myself to hell.*

"No," Dorry told her parents. "I want to stay here."

She'd overheard her parents talking about counseling, her father muttering, "Those psychiatrist types are all a bunch of fools!" and her mother protesting, "But just look at her—" Seeing her watching them, her mother twittered, "Dorry, is there anyone at school who can help you? Someone you'd trust—"

"No," Dorry said. "No one."

She wanted to go back to Fishers, she ached to go back, she wanted to have all of them and God love her again. But every time she reached for the phone or saw Angela in the hall, the vision of Zoe's and Jasmine's tortured faces swam up before her eyes.

Now she stared vacantly at the milk leaking from her carton where the seams didn't meet evenly.

"Know what happens to fish who get caught?" a male voice said suddenly in her ear. "They die."

Dorry looked up. She blinked at the boy who sat down beside her. His name came to her out of memories that seemed buried a hundred years back. Zachary. He'd been at the retreat with her. He'd been at the E-Team meeting. The first one. Had she seen him after that?

"I'm not a Fisher anymore," she said dully. "You're not allowed to talk to me."

"Sure I am," Zachary countered. "You don't think I'm still in that crooked outfit, do you? That's why I asked you that riddle. Think about it. We were called Fishers because Jesus said that thing about his followers being fishers of men. But it's a lousy metaphor, because in nature, if you're a fish, it's really a bummer to be caught. It's death."

Dorry blinked again. "I never thought of that," she said. "Not once." It changed something. She wasn't sure how.

Zachary sat back and drummed his fingers on the table, one hand reaching over the other to make an imaginary cymbal crash at the end.

"That's okay," he said. "You haven't been out as long as me. And in Fishers—whoa. They do everything to keep you from thinking."

Dorry looked closely at Zachary. The wimpy, tortured kid she remembered from the E-Team meeting was gone, replaced by a peppy guy in constant motion, tapping his feet, bobbing his head, grinning. Dorry's brain, well trained, cranked out, "The old has passed away, behold, the new has come." Second Corinthians 5:17. But this had happened in reverse. The old Zachary had been the holy one. The new one was—evil?

"I've got to say," Zachary continued, "I didn't peg you as someone who would leave. I thought you were fully convicted."

"I was," Dorry said quietly. But had she been? She remembered the doubts she'd swallowed, the rebellious words she'd held back at practically every discipling session.

"So what happened?"

Briefly, Dorry told him about her botched attempt at converting the Garringer kids.

"Now, see, you've got drama," Zachary congratulated her when she was done. "I just had all these doubts building in me until one day I looked at my discipler and said, 'You're full of it.'"

"And that was the end?" Dorry asked.

"Haven't looked back since," he announced proudly.

"Even when they called and called and—"

"The harassment, you mean? I just started arguing with them. Even talked one other guy into quitting with me. Believe me, they gave up real quick after that."

"Oh," Dorry said.

"Some kids, though—did you hear about the girl who ended up in the mental hospital? Lara somebody?"

Dorry searched for the last name she knew. "French?"

Zachary nodded. "Yeah. Know her? Sad case. She was so fervent, she wanted to convert everybody on the planet, but she wouldn't play by the Fishers' rules, following the exact procedure, letting the top level Fishers get the credit for every convert—"

Poor Lara, Dorry thought. She remembered Lara and Angela fighting. Of course there'd been no stolen necklace, no kleptomania. They had been fighting over her, she realized now, without a single ounce of surprise. But, oh, how she'd wanted to believe everything Angela told her. "Everybody likes you. You know that, don't you?"

"So when this Lara finally gave up, the top Fishers were merciless," Zachary explained. "Her mother told me she had a nervous breakdown. That's one of the things I reported."

"Reported?" Dorry asked.

Zachary looked around. "Yeah . . . I can tell you lots more. But I don't want to waste this. Let's sit somewhere else. Come on."

He stood up, picked up his tray, and walked to another chair several tables away. Dorry mustered the energy to follow him.

"What was that for?" she asked when she caught up with him. He shoved out a chair for her on the other side of the table.

238

"I'll explain later," he said. "Now I'm going to tell you everything about Fishers you should have known going in."

Dorry waited.

"First of all, it's a cult. I did a lot of research right after I left, and checked with some anti-cult groups, and they were *very* interested. Fishers meets every single one of their defining criteria." Zachary spoke loudly, as if he wanted the whole cafeteria to hear.

He waited for response from Dorry. When she said nothing, he added, "Don't you understand? You were in a cult."

It was just a word to Dorry. "So I was really stupid and fell for something crazy," she said. "My parents have been telling me that all along. And I keep thinking, sure, but lots of people believe in God. Lots of people believe in Jesus. They just don't practice their faith the right way."

"According to Fishers," Zachary said. "See? You were brainwashed. It's not so much what Fishers believe that's wrong, as how they make you believe it. They manipulate and harass and require complete obedience. They claim to be perfect and without sin, but they'll lie and cheat and do anything to keep their members in line."

Dorry remembered Angela's lies. "They say they only lie when it suits God's purposes. When its God's will," Dorry protested.

"But only they know God's will, right?"

Reluctantly Dorry nodded. "But if they sincerely believe they're doing the right thing—" Dorry didn't know why she felt compelled to defend the Fishers.

Zachary cocked his head. "I'll grant you that some of the people are sincere. They do think they're serving God. But there's so much that's fake, that no one who's in the group very long could continue to be fooled. You remember that girl who saw God that first night at our retreat?"

"Moira," Dorry said. She closed her eyes momentarily, remembering how awed she felt witnessing Moira's dramatic conversion. Why hadn't Dorry's own faith been so simple?

"Made an impression, didn't it?" Zachary said. "Only problem was, it was all a sham. I mean, Moira'd been a Fisher for three years. She was just acting. They have someone perform like that at every retreat."

Dorry gasped. "How do you know?"

"I ask questions." Zachary sat back with a self-satisfied smirk.

"But—"

Zachary wasn't about to be interrupted. "And didn't you notice the pattern of it all? In the beginning, everything was so happy and joyous. Everybody loved everybody else and God was like Santa Claus and weren't you just dying to be around these people who thought of nothing but you?"

Dorry looked down. "Yes," she whispered.

"That's called love bombing, incidentally, in cult terminology," Zachary said. "But then there's a whole cycle of membership after that. They can't be loving to everybody all the time because they need to save their energy for recruiting new members. Once they're sure they've gotten you, they have this big ceremony and tell you what a great person you are, you're now a Level Two, and then everything gets intense. They give you orders they know you'll fail at, nearly impossible things, so that you'll feel guilty, and try even harder to please them."

Eyes downcast, Dorry admitted, "Angela made it seem like I did something wrong because I couldn't convert my parents. She was always expecting me to convert people. And she told me to fast on Thanksgiving, even though we were having a huge family dinner."

That seemed to surprise even Zachary.

"Really?" he said. "That's truly cruel. Did you?"

"Sort of," Dorry said. Familiar shame flooded over her. But now, she wasn't sure if she was ashamed of failing to fast or ashamed of trying to. Either way, remembering Thanksgiving made her want to cry. "I don't want to talk about it."

"Fine," Zachary said. "But you have to see the pattern,

how things intensified. They were trying to shake out the iffy believers, the ones who weren't fully committed, so they'd have a core group of devout, brainwashed people willing to do anything for the cause."

Dorry thought of nearly being arrested at the mall. "But why?" she asked, truly bewildered. "Why create this—this whole kingdom—if it's not for God?"

Zachary snorted. "You really were an easy mark for Fishers, weren't you, Miss Gullible?" He shook his head. "Sorry. I thought you were smarter than that. Ever notice the offering plate at Fishers services?"

"Sure, but—"

"Pastor Jim's got a lot of money, thanks to Fishers. He's got practically a mansion up in Carmel—" Dorry wasn't ready to believe that. "No, he's got an apartment in a bad part of the city. He talks about it all the time."

"That's just for show. Or reverse show. You didn't give a lot of money to Fishers, did you?"

Dorry looked away. "My college savings," she said.

Zachary didn't say anything for a minute. Dorry saw that a group of boys sitting nearby were stirring about, looking disturbed.

"At least you didn't sleep with him. Did you?" Zachary asked.

"What?" Dorry stopped watching the other boys and jerked her attention back to Zachary. "Of course not.

242

Everyone in Fishers says premarital sex is wrong."

Zachary laughed in a way that made Dorry feel like crying. "Sure, that's what they *say*," he said. "But Pastor Jim probably had half the girls in Fishers. That Angela who was your discipler—I think she was one of his favorites."

"That's ridiculous," Dorry said. But she remembered the spark Angela had had with Pastor Jim at that first party, the looks that had traveled between them.

"He tells girls it's their sacrifice for God," Zachary said.

Dorry could imagine Pastor Jim saying that, could picture his mouth forming those words. And then did everyone comply? Why had he never asked her? *Too ugly*, a voice said in her head. *Someone who could have any girl in Fishers wouldn't have wanted you.* She felt rejected all over again. Shouldn't she feel relieved instead? She struggled to keep her expression neutral, to act like Zachary's words didn't bother her. Zachary wasn't even watching.

"Meanwhile, all the new male Fishers are told abstinence is sacred, that they mustn't even think of girls or they will burn in hell," he said. "Aren't you, guys?"

Zachary spoke over Dorry's shoulder, directing his voice to the group of boys behind her. They whispered among themselves, then each of them shoved out his chair and stood up, almost in synchronicity. They all but marched past Zachary and Dorry, their heads held high, eyes straight ahead. Only one scrawny, nervous-looking boy darted his eyes toward Zachary and Dorry. Then he quickly looked away.

Zachary laughed and laughed. "Can't bear hearing the truth, huh?" he shouted after them.

One of the boys—a tall, imposing guy, more muscular than many football players Dorry had seen—turned around and walked back. He leaned both hands on the table beside Dorry and looked down at Zachary. The table groaned. "Zachary Haines, you are filled with evil," he said in a booming voice. "You have ensured your place in hell by trying to tempt new believers. But you will not triumph."

It scared Dorry, and she wasn't even the one being condemned. Zachary only laughed harder. "You guys really have to come up with some new threats," he shot back. "That hell thing is getting old."

The muscular guy didn't respond. He glanced once at Dorry—dismissively, like she was an insect or some other creature without a soul to go to heaven or hell. Then he turned with military precision and walked away.

Zachary kept chuckling. "In case you didn't figure it out," he said. "That was a new Bible Study group. Guess we shook them up, huh?"

Dorry wanted to slap him. "Give me some credit,"

she snapped. "I'm not that stupid. You were baiting them. You just told me all that to get to them. You made it all up. You're worse than the Fishers. At least some of them believe in what they do."

Then she pushed away from the table. With much less dignity than the Fishers had shown, she walked away from Zachary.

"Wait!" he yelled. "Dorry, wait!"

Dorry turned around. What did she have to lose? Zachary rushed up behind her. "I'm sorry. Nobody else I did that to thought it was wrong, to bait the Fishers. They were all happy to find out the truth."

"Oh, yeah?" Dorry said. "Maybe they're just used to being manipulated." But her anger was already fizzling. She leaned against the wall. "Was that the truth?" she asked.

Zachary nodded. "I think so. I can't verify everything, but I did look up Pastor Jim's property records—I'm not making up the mansion. The sex stuff I heard about from some of the other girls who left."

"How do you know they're not lying?"

"I don't," he admitted. He looked down. "Maybe you're right. Maybe I'm too biased. I've got too much to prove. I'm trying to get Fishers put on official lists of known cults. I'm trying to get the school to ban them from recruiting on campus. I'm trying to get the police to check into Pastor Jim's finances, because I'm sure he's embezzling. I think something's about to happen, because Fishers seems to be getting more extreme by the day. I'm—"

Zachary stopped only because Dorry laughed.

"Didn't you just tell me that you left Fishers and never looked back?" she asked. A group of kids walked past and looked at her and Zachary curiously. Dorry ignored them. She'd gotten used to being looked at strangely in Fishers.

Zachary smiled wryly. "Okay, okay, you've got me. I'm obsessed. But don't you want to see Fishers destroyed? For what they did to you and to me and to that Lara girl and everyone else?"

Dorry hesitated. She looked out at the cafeteria, at the vast ocean of kids she'd felt lost and anonymous in, before Fishers. "No," she said at last. "I want them to be as good and nice and pure as they pretended to be in the beginning. I want to have the love and the sense of belonging Fishers promised me. And the holiness." She held her breath, scared Zachary would laugh. He didn't.

"But you can't," Zachary said. "That's just—idealism."

"Uh-huh," Dorry said. "Isn't that what religion's for?"

Zachary squinted. "But religion's evil."

"No," Dorry said. "Fishers was. Religion isn't."

And for the first time since leaving Angela's car, Dorry felt a glimmer of the peace—and the rightness, the righteousness—she'd experienced when she first joined Fishers.

"You know what?" she told Zachary. "I just realized—when I left Fishers, I didn't leave God. I left because of God. He wanted me to. I kept praying and praying and praying, trying to stop rebelling against Angela. But it was God telling me to rebel. Not the Devil."

Zachary stared at her as though she had just announced she was a new messiah, come to battle Pastor Jim and his Fishers for the souls of Crestwood. "You're crazy, too," he said.

The bell marking the end of lunch period suddenly rang, sending kids scurrying around them. Dorry stood still.

"No," she told Zachary. "I'm finally sane."

CHAPTER TWENTY-EIGHT

DORRY LIFTED THE FAMILIAR brass knocker and hesitated. This wasn't going to be easy. She let the knocker fall. Once it struck the door, there was no turning back.

In a few moments she heard sounds of a familiar frenzy, Zoe shouting, "Mom-mee! Someone's at the door!" But there were unfamiliar sounds, too: barking and a dog's toenails scratching on the hardwood floor, and an unfamiliar woman's voice calling, "Do you want me to get that, Mrs. Garringer?"

Soon the door creaked open and there was Mrs. Garringer. "Dorry." she said, neither welcoming nor turning her away, just acknowledging she was there.

"I came to apolo—" Dorry started, but couldn't finish because suddenly a big golden retriever jumped at the door, and Zoe cowered behind Mrs. Garringer screaming, "It's Dorry! Mommy, make her go away!"

"Strudel, down," Mrs. Garringer commanded the dog. "Zoe, it's okay. Nothing's going to happen. I'm going to talk to Dorry now. Why don't you and Strudel go watch TV with Jasmine and Mrs. Faunt?" She gave Zoe and the dog a little push for emphasis and the two trotted away, Zoe clinging to the dog's hair.

"Well," Mrs. Garringer said, facing Dorry through the screen door as if deciding something. "Want to come on back to my studio? It's quiet there."

Silently, Dorry trailed behind Mrs. Garringer, everything she'd planned to say bubbling in her head. In wild moments she'd had hopes of being received like the Prodigal Son, the kids jumping over her with delight. Obviously that hadn't happened. But neither had her greatest fear—Mrs. Garringer hadn't refused to speak to her, or slammed the door in her face.

In the studio, Dorry stopped in surprise. Ahead of her was a huge sculpture, almost as tall as the ceiling, and as wide as the Stevenses' kitchen table. It wasn't shaped like anything—Dorry could tell it wasn't supposed to be a human or a tree or anything real. But the swirls running up and down and twisting along the entire piece conveyed such a sense of power and majesty that Dorry thought of a phrase from the Bible: "Be still and know that I am God."

"I never saw what you were working on," she said in awe. "I didn't know it was—this."

"No. I didn't show it to anybody for a long time. I always draped it before letting anyone in." She laughed. "Anyhow, I figured you might think it was a graven image or something."

Dorry turned to face Mrs. Garringer. "I left Fishers," she said. "Right after—you know. I'm really sorry about what happened. I was wrong to tell your kids about hell. I haven't been able to stop thinking about it."

Mrs. Garringer accepted the apology with a curt nod. "I thought you would be sorry. I've felt bad, too, about the way I handled things. But you really spooked the kids and my mother-bear instinct came out—"

"They're okay now, aren't they?" Dorry asked anxiously.

Mrs. Garringer waved her hand toward a pair of stools, indicating Dorry should sit down. Dorry sat, and so did Mrs. Garringer.

"Want something to drink? A Coke? Coffee?"

"No, thanks," Dorry said. "Are the kids okay now?"

Mrs. Garringer sipped from a clay-caked cup of coffee that looked like it had been sitting there for days. "Mostly. They had nightmares for a long time—I wasn't too happy with you the third or fourth night Zoe woke me up screaming at three a.m. You had bad timing, because our neighbor's house had burned down the week before. I don't know, maybe they would have had nightmares anyway. But we got the dog, and now they think Strudel will protect them—my husband wanted an excuse to get a dog anyway."

"Oh," Dorry said. She looked around. The back of Mrs. Garringer's studio was a row of windows facing the spacious backyard. Dorry saw dozens of trees full of new, unfolding leaves.

"So you left Fishers," Mrs. Garringer said. "My neighbors—remember the Murrins?—they did, too. I thought you might. You didn't have scary eyes like that friend of yours."

"Angela?" Dorry asked.

"Yes. She gave me the creeps. I almost didn't hire you because she bothered me so much. And then when you left the room that first day, she told me a long story about how you needed the money to pay for your mother's medical care, but you didn't want people to know you were so poor . . . I didn't think it was true. Was it?"

"No," Dorry said, burning with shame. "Why didn't you ask me about it before?"

Mrs. Garringer shrugged. "I would have if you'd made it a little easier for me. But you never seemed to want to talk."

Dorry remembered how uncomfortable she'd always

felt around Mrs. Garringer, how antisocial she must have seemed. She knew now that she'd been afraid Mrs. Garringer would say something to make her question Fishers.

She gulped. "Why did you hire me?"

"I thought you'd be good with the kids. Your references recommended you highly. I was desperate. And, I figured, I'd be right here the whole time, so if anything happened, I could stop it." She frowned ruefully. "So much for my plans."

Dorry thought about Zoe running hysterically to her mother. "I'm sorry," she said again.

Mrs. Garringer took another sip of coffee. "There was an upside to all of this," she said. "I was a little distressed to find out Jasmine thought God was imaginary, like Santa Claus. So we've been talking about religion, what other people believe."

"What do you believe?" Dorry asked.

"Oh, I'm still figuring that out. What about you?"

"The same," Dorry said. She and Mrs. Garringer laughed together. "I believe . . . I believe it's important to find out. I still believe in God, just not the sick and twisted version Fishers gave me."

"Sick and twisted" was a Zachary description. Dorry stopped to think if she was just parroting him, or if she agreed.

"So have you found another version you like? Or are you going to make something up on your own?" Mrs. Garringer asked, as if God were just a piece of art you could sculpt however you wanted.

Dorry frowned. "Its more like, I pray a lot, asking God how I should see Him, what I should do. And I read the Bible, trying to understand what it means, why it has so many contradictions. It's a lot harder than Fishers, where someone always told me what to do and what to believe."

Mrs. Garringer cocked her head thoughtfully. "Are you doing this alone?"

"No," Dorry said. "I have a friend, Zachary, who left Fishers, too. We kind of balance each other out. He wants to expose Fishers, and I'm his fact checker, making him investigate things, instead of believing every bad thing people say about Fishers. And I'm making him think about what he wants to stand for, instead of just automatically opposing everything about Fishers. Then he challenges everything I consider believing. He says he doesn't want me to fall for the Moonies or something next." Dorry grinned to let Mrs. Garringer know that wasn't likely.

"And we've gotten a group of other former Fishers together, to talk about what we went through and what we believe now. We're going to invite religious experts and psychologists and stuff in to talk to us. Zachary wants to call us 'The Ones Who Got Away'—playing on the fishing theme, you know? I'm lobbying for 'Seekers,' because it's not just about leaving Fishers, but finding something else."

"Seekers of Truth?" Mrs. Garringer proposed.

"No," Dorry said. "'Truth' is too—" She couldn't come up with the right word. Hard-edged? Extreme? Absolute? She thought about the first meeting of the former Fishers. Even Lara had been there, looking lost and pitiful. The others had made Dorry feel downright stable and self-assured. But maybe she was now. She wanted to convey that to Mrs. Garringer, to let her know that she'd brought her grades back up to mostly As instead of mostly Cs, that her parents weren't worried about her anymore, that there was no more talk of sending her back to Bryden.

"Anyhow," Dorry said. "I wanted you to know that I'm not, uh, fanatical anymore. And I'm really, really sorry about what happened."

Mrs. Garringer nodded thoughtfully. There was a pause, with Mrs. Garringer drinking more coffee and Dorry looking down at her hands folded on Mrs. Garringer's paint-splattered table.

"Dorry," Mrs. Garringer said. "I can't give you your job back. I hired someone else, and anyhow, I don't think it would work. I can't—well, I can't trust you anymore."

"I know," Dorry said, swallowing hard. "I didn't expect you to." But, even saying that, she knew that somehow she had. She had thought that she could erase all the problems Fishers had caused her, and just carry away the good things she'd learned. But of course life didn't work that way. She looked out at the Garringers' trees again, the thousands and thousands of new green buds.

"Can I tell the kids I'm sorry?" she asked. After a moment, Mrs. Garringer nodded. They went out to the family room, and Dorry knelt in front of Zoe and Jasmine. Mrs. Faunt, an older, heavyset woman, sat beside them knitting, while Seth played with her ball of yarn.

"I'm sorry I scared you the last time I was here," Dorry told the girls.

"That was bad," Zoe insisted gravely. "You're bad."

"No," Dorry said. "And yes. I'm good and bad both. Everybody is."

Zoe looked puzzled, but then she threw her arms around Dorry and laughed. "I still like you," she said. "You're good."

Dorry felt the little girl's arms around her shoulders, and then, as if it were a competition to see who loved Dorry more, Jasmine hugged her, too. For a minute Dorry wished she could see the world the way Zoe did: good, bad, black, white, no shadows, no grays, no half one thing and half another.

But she'd tried that in Fishers and it hadn't worked. Life wasn't that easy—or that hard.

THE ALWAYS WAR

For as long as Tessa can remember, her country has been at war. When local golden boy Gideon Thrall is awarded a medal for courage, it's a rare bright spot for everyone in Tessa's town—until Gideon refuses the award, claims he was a coward, and runs away. Tessa is bewildered, and can't help but follow Gideon to find out the truth. But Tessa is in for more than she bargained for. Before she knows it, she has stowed away on a rogue airplane and is headed for enemy territory. But all that pales when she discovers a shocking truth that rocks the foundation of everything she's ever believed—a truth that will change the world. But is Tessa strong enough to bring it into the light?

Available now from Simon & Schuster

Gideon Thrall stood offstage, waiting in the wings. The announcer hadn't called his name yet, but people craned their necks and leaned sideways to see him. Whispers of excitement began to float through the crowd: "There he is!" "The hero . . ." "Doesn't he just *look* like a hero?"

Then the PA system boomed out, so loudly that the words seemed to be part of Tessa's brain: "And now, our honoree, the young man we will be forever indebted to for our survival, for our very way of life—Lieutenant-Pilot Gideon Thrall!"

The applause thundered through the crowd. Gideon took his first steps into the spotlight. His golden hair gleamed, every strand perfectly in place. His white uniform, perfectly creased, glowed against the darkness around him. He could have been an angel, a saint—some creature who stood above ordinary humans. Even the fact that he walked humbly, with his head bowed, was perfect. At a moment like this most people would have looked too proud, like they were gloating. But not Gideon. He wasn't going to lord it over anyone that he, Gideon Thrall, had just won his nation's highest honor, something nobody else from Waterford City had ever done.

Standing at the back of the crowd with the other kids from the common school, Tessa felt her heart swell with pride.

"I know him," she whispered.

The applause had just begun to taper off, so Tessa's voice rang out louder than she'd intended. It was actually audible. Down the row Cordina Kurdle fixed Tessa with a hard stare.

"What did you say, flea?" Cordina asked.

Tessa knew better than to repeat her boast. The safe response would be a shrug, a cowed shake of the head, maybe a mumbled, "Nothing. Sorry for bothering you." But sometimes something got into her, some bold recklessness she couldn't explain.

Maybe she wanted to brag more than she wanted to be safe?

"I said, I know him." She cleared her throat. "He was my neighbor. We grew up together."

Cordina snorted.

"Hear that?" she said to the kids clustered around her.

Her sycophants, Tessa thought. *Cronies. Henchmen.*

The words she'd found in old books were fun to think about, but they wouldn't provide much protection if Cordina decided that someone needed to beat up Tessa to teach her a lesson.

"Hear what?" one of the sycophants asked, right on cue.

"Gnat over there thinks she deserves some credit for

living on the same planet as the hero," Cordina mocked.

"We were next-door neighbors," Tessa said. She stopped herself from adding, *We made mud pies together when we were little*, though it was true. Possibly. Tessa didn't remember it herself, but way back when Gideon was first chosen for the military academy, Tessa's mother had started showing around a picture of Tessa, about age two, and Gideon, age five or six, playing together in the mud behind their apartment building.

Gideon had looked like a golden child destined for great things even then, even sitting in mud.

Tessa had looked . . . muddy.

Tessa was saved from any further temptation to brag—or embarrass herself—because the general who'd come from the capital just for this occasion stepped to the podium. He held up a medallion on a chain, and the whole auditorium grew quiet. The general let the medallion swing back and forth, ever so slightly, and the spotlight glinted from it out into the crowd. For a moment Tessa forgot that the city auditorium was squalid and dirty and full of broken chairs and cracked flooring. For a moment she forgot that the people in the crowd had runny noses and blotchy skin and patched clothing. She forgot they could be so mean and low-down. For that one moment everyone shared in the light.

"Courage," the general said in a hushed voice, as if he too were in awe. "We give this medal of honor for courage far above the measure of ordinary citizens. Only eleven people have earned this medal in our nation's history. And now Gideon Thrall, a proud son of Waterford City, will be the twelfth." He turned. "Gideon?"

The general lifted the chain even higher, ready to slip it over Gideon's head. Gideon took a halting step forward, as if he wasn't quite sure what he was supposed to do.

No, Tessa thought. To her surprise she was suddenly furious with Gideon. *Don't hesitate now! Be bold! You're getting an award for courage. Act like it!*

Gideon was staring at the medallion. Even from the back of the auditorium Tessa could see his face twist into an expression that looked nothing like boldness or bravery. How could he be acting so confused? Or . . . scared?

"For your bravery in battle," the general said, holding out the medallion like a beacon. He was trying to guide Gideon into place. Gideon just needed to put his head inside the chain. Then everyone could clap and cheer again, and all the awkwardness would be forgotten.

Gideon made no move toward the chain.

"No," Gideon said, and in the silent auditorium his voice sounded weak and panicky. "I . . . can't."

"Can't?" the general repeated, clearly unable to believe his own ears.

"I don't deserve it," Gideon said, and strangely, his voice was stronger now. "I wasn't brave. I was a coward."

He looked at the general, looked at the medallion—and whirled around and ran from the auditorium.

Some loves are worth dying for.

Others are worth killing for.

Love is lost but never forgotten . . .

Don't miss the *elixir* series
by New York Times bestselling author
HILARY DUFF